TURNED OUT! AND BLACK BRA AND PANTIES
Two Novels of Hardcore Erotica

TURNED OUT! AND BLACK BRA AND PANTIES
Two Novels of Hardcore Erotica

REGGIE CHESTERFIELD

ABERNATHY AND MONROE

For the appreciators.

This edition published in 2010 by Abernathy and Monroe.

Turned Out! copyright © 2003 by Reggie Chesterfield.
Black Bra and Panties copyright © 2003 by Reggie Chesterfield.

Paperback ISBN-13: 978-0-9845352-3-1
Paperback ISBN-10: 0-9845352-3-3

First published by New Tradition Books in 2003.

eBook ISBN–13: 978-0-9845352-4-8
eBook ISBN–10: 0-9845352-4-1

This book is a work of fiction. Names, characters, places and incidents are either the product of the author's imagination or are used fictitiously. Any resemblance to actual events or locales or persons, living or dead is entirely coincidental.

Turned Out!

1

Julie anxiously hurried around her dorm room getting ready to go over to her boyfriend's place. Even though she and Dave had been going out for over a year, it wasn't like she was trying to make a good impression or anything. She had already done that, or at least she hoped she had. No, the reason why everything had to be just right was that she was sure Dave was going to ask her to marry him. The notion both excited and frightened her.

Her roommate, Josie, looked on with amusement.

"So, why all the fuss? Don't you see this guy all the time?" the slender redhead said as she lit a cigarette. Not taking her eyes off Julie, she reclined back on her bed, getting comfortable in the tight leather pants she intended to wear to a club a little later that evening. The pants fit better if she put them on a little earlier than the rest of her outfit. This way, they had plenty of time to contour to her body. Wearing only the pants and a bra, she looked like something out of a perfume ad. Actually, she had modeled a few times, but it wasn't for anything like that. Her pictures had been featured in such *gentlemen's* magazines as *Scoundrel* and *Black Bra and Panties*. She had never told Julie about that stuff, though. She didn't think Julie would understand. And, more than likely, she was right.

Julie sighed. "I think Dave is going to ask me to marry him tonight."

Josie rolled her eyes. Being a party girl, she never really understood how Julie could be such a prude. Especially considering the fact that Julie was such a knockout. She had never met anyone so sweet and naïve. And so pretty. No, pretty wasn't the right word for her. It didn't do her justice. She was absolutely gorgeous. She was the kind of girl who always got the attention of everyone in the room, male *or* female. Josie often found herself staring at the pretty brunette. Julie's blue eyes were breathtaking and her body was amazing. She was just perfect. This was something coming from a girl like Josie who was no slouch in the looks department herself.

Josie sometimes had to make herself look away so Julie wouldn't think she was creepy. She often had fantasies where she would be on a photo shoot with Julie and she would pull out a double-headed dildo and they would fuck each other silly while they took pictures and made money. To her making money was almost as much fun as having sex. Just thinking about that kind of stuff made the redhead wet and she couldn't help but cross and uncross her long legs at the thought of them scissoring Julie's pussy. She licked her lips just thinking about the taste of it and felt her fingers creeping down her stomach. She stopped herself before she could go any further, lest she embarrass herself. She took another drag off her cigarette and tried to remain composed.

Julie didn't seem to notice anything awry and continued. "I want this night to be perfect. I've been waiting for this all my life. I just have to wear the right outfit."

She held up a little sun dress. The dress was blue, went down about knee length and showed absolutely no cleavage, much to Josie's disappointment. She just didn't understand the girl.

"What do you think about this? Do you think it's too...*revealing*?"

Josie tried hard not to roll her eyes again. The sun dress was in no way revealing, at least not intentionally.

"Haven't you worn that dress to church?"

Julie giggled. "Yes, but..."

"Then why do you think it's too revealing?"

"I don't know. I guess it's because it shows my arms."

Josie shook her head slightly in disbelief. What could she say to Julie that would make her realize what a beauty she was? Well, nothing. She didn't want to risk being found out. Julie was not the kind of girl who would understand a same sex crush. Unfortunately.

Julie smiled and sat down on the bed beside Josie. "I'm sorry I'm being such a lame-brain about this, I'm just so nervous. I just know he's gonna ask me."

Josie moved a little closer to Julie. She couldn't believe that Julie could be so dorky. Regardless, she was no less attracted to her. Josie looked at her hair and couldn't resist playing with it.

Julie moved her head a little closer to Josie. She loved for her hair to be played with and was oblivious to the redhead's advances. Josie began to think that maybe this would be the day that Julie would let her do more than just play with her hair. She put a hand on the girl's shoulder and began giving her a gentle massage.

"So, what are you going to do about school if you get married?" Josie asked, feeling herself becoming wet due to the proximity of the pretty brunette. She was breathing a little more rapidly now. The smell of Julie's perfume was intoxicating and she could imagine kissing the girl's neck softly. She could imagine the moan that would escape her full lips. Imagining that made Josie want to move a little closer to her. Julie didn't notice.

"Dave's gonna pay for it. Once we're married, I'll be able to quit my job at the mall and concentrate on school...and Dave." She giggled.

"Sounds great," Josie murmured, moving a little closer to Julie. She could almost feel the firmness of Julie's breasts and the moistness of her lips. She moved her hand along Julie's shoulder, and down her collarbone, but before she had a chance to proceed, Julie jumped up.

"Gosh, I've got to hurry. I'm gonna be late," Julie said and hurriedly dashed around, getting herself ready.

Josie sighed a lit another cigarette. She guessed she would just have to be content with masturbating to fantasies of Julie until it was time to leave for the club.

Again.

2

Later that night, there was a tension so thick in Dave's apartment it could have been cut with a knife. His breathing was audible as he nervously pulled the box from his pocket and got down on one knee. The feeling of romance was heavy in the air. He had made sure of that. He and Julie were surrounded by blazing candles he had placed all around the living room. Maybe it was a bit much, but from the look in Julie's eye, he could tell it was far from overkill. She loved stuff like that. And he loved her.

I do, I do love her, Dave thought to himself. He had utilized every trick at his disposal. He had the aromatherapy going. He had the rose petals. He had everything. He just hoped it would work. Living another day without her was just not an option at this point. She was in his blood now. He loved her that much.

"Will you marry me?" Dave looked up at Julie like a puppy dog, begging for approval.

Julie held her breath as she watched her premonition unfold. On bended knee, he held the ring out. She smiled down at him; he was so cute. How could he possibly think that she was going to say no?

"Of course, I will!" Julie exclaimed, hugging Dave and giving him a deep kiss. She was so happy. This is what she had been waiting for all her life. To get married to the guy she loved. She had been planning the wedding for years. There would be lots of flowers, food, bridesmaids, groomsmen, flower girls and horses. Yes, horses. She had always dreamed of riding up to the church in a romantic horse drawn carriage.

Dave breathed a sigh of relief. This made him pretty happy, too. There was a moment there that he thought she might reply in the negative. And why wouldn't she? Here he was, Joe Average, wanting to marry the prettiest girl in town. That kind of stuff didn't happen everyday. Whenever he looked at her, he couldn't believe he was so lucky. He never really understood what she saw in him, but apparently it was something he didn't. But he wasn't going to argue with her.

"I've got to call my mom!" Julie squealed.

She pulled away from him and skipped to the phone. While she talked to her mother, Dave watched the beautiful girl. His first worry was about money. He knew it was going to be tight. Julie managed an accessory shop at the mall part-time and he was bottom of the totem pole at a dot com corporation. He knew things would get better and that he just had to give them a little time to do so. He had skills that he had learned in the service and he was still young. They would be okay. But then... No. He didn't want to think about anything but his happiness at that moment. No need to ruin it with ideas of her leaving him for a richer or better man. He would do that after they were married.

"Mom was so excited," she said, hanging up the phone. "She said that I couldn't have picked a better guy."

Dave smiled. This made him feel all warm and fuzzy. He was even more pleased with himself for being in love with such a wonderful person.

"Aren't you gonna tell anyone about it?" she asked.

He sat up. "You're right! This is one of the most important moments in my life. I just have to tell someone!"

He picked up the phone and called his parents. The phone rang and rang and rang. No one was home. He wasn't surprised because this was what happened whenever he called. No one ever answered. The answering machine clicked on after four rings. He really didn't want to leave a message, so he hung up and resolved to call later, though the thought slightly irked him. His parents were never around for any of the important stuff.

He sat there fuming at the phone for a moment.

"You can call them later. Why don't you come over here and sit next to me?" Julie purred.

"No, damn it! I've got to tell someone."

He picked up the phone and started dialing again. This time he called his sister. Again, no answer.

"Damn! Nobody's home. I wish I knew more people in town. I'm just busting to tell someone."

"How about calling that guy you know...you know that one you talk about sometimes? He doesn't sound like he goes out much. Maybe he'll be home."

Dave stared at her for a moment, then realized who she was talking about. Charlie. Charlie would answer his phone. He was about the only person Dave knew who would.

"Oh, yeah, I guess I could," Dave said and began to dial his number.

It took a little while for Charlie to pick up and after he finally did, Dave knew what had taken him so long. From the sounds coming from the room, it sounded as if there was an orgy going on.

"Hello..."

"I didn't call you at a bad time, did I?" Dave asked.

"Well, yeah, Dave. I'm fucking a couple of chicks."

"Do you want me to let you go?"

"Nah, that's okay, one of 'em is gonna keep giving me head while I'm on the phone."

Dave whistled to himself. That Charlie sure was a character. However, he was just too excited to keep the good news from him.

"I'm engaged!" he blurted. "Can you believe it?!"

Unfortunately, Charlie's reaction wasn't what he intended. As they talked about the engagement and Julie, Dave's face darkened.

"You're kidding?" Charlie asked.

"Uh, no, why would I be kidding?"

"Well, okay, then. If that's what you want," Charlie said matter of factly.

Dave stared at the phone for an instant before replying, "Yes, this is what I want."

Julie smiled over at him. It took him a moment before he smiled back.

"Really?" Charlie said.

"Yes, really."

"I don't believe that."

Dave really couldn't believe Charlie was being such a dick, but he decided not to let his apparent lack of interest (or support) darken the happiest moment of his life. Charlie was of the opinion that once you were married, you were dead. Or at least your sex life was. Dave listened as Charlie rambled on about how Julie would "freeze" up once the ring was on her finger. He gave Dave a detailed prediction of what his sex life would be like *after* the wedding.

"You might as well get neutered, because you sure as hell ain't gonna be getting any."

"Thanks for all your support, Charlie," Dave grumbled.

"I'm just trying to let you know is all," he drawled.

"You're a real bastard."

"You'll find out," Charlie said smugly.

"I'll let you get back to whatever it was you're doing." Dave said angrily and hung up the phone.

"What did he think?" Julie asked sweetly.

"Oh, he was just congratulating me," Dave said, trying to sound cheerful.

"Well, that was sweet," she said and gave him a little kiss on the cheek.

Dave sighed. Yeah. Real sweet.

She stood up and walked towards the bedroom, then stopped and motioned for him to follow her.

"You coming or not?"

Dave smiled and let the anger dissolve. To hell with Charlie anyway. What did he know? He couldn't wait to get his hands on Julie's tight little body again. He followed her into the bedroom where she waited seductively on the bed.

"Dave?" she said as he began to kiss her neck.

"Yes, Julie?"

"Would you please turn the lights off? We really need to get some sleep."

Dave sighed. He got up and turned the lights off. Charlie   was right. It was already beginning.

3

After Julie left later that night, Dave thought about what Charlie had said on the phone. The thing that troubled him most was not the disinterest, but rather the part about his sex life. He knew, to a certain extent, that Charlie was right. And that bothered him.

He decided to swallow his pride and called Charlie back. They met at an all-night diner.

Charlie was already sitting in a booth near the back drinking coffee and eating a slice of cherry pie when Dave arrived. Charlie and Dave had gone to high school together and had later enlisted in the Marines at the same time. They had once been pretty close, but since Dave had started seeing Julie, they had grown apart. Dave, of course, knew that Charlie resented the fact that Julie had come between them. This was one of the reasons why he had never introduced him to her. As a result, he wasn't surprised that Charlie had said the things he had said over the phone, however, his interest was a little piqued.

"Why did you say that I might as well be neutered?" Dave asked.

"Because it's true," Charlie explained. "If you don't stay drunk all the time or cheat on her, you're gonna have blue balls the size of cantaloupes."

"Come on!" Dave said. "I really don't know about that, Charlie. Julie really doesn't seem like that kind of girl. I mean, we really don't do it that much now, so it would seem that she would really loosen up after we're married."

At that, Charlie really started cackling.

"Dude, c'mon. I've been married. It doesn't work like that. At first, she might be a little wilder than usual because she's not worried about her mother catching her or she's drunk with the freedom of living on her own, under her own rules, but it won't last long. As soon as the bills start rolling in and you two aren't spending every waking moment together, she'll start having a little bit more time to think. And brother, you ain't gonna like what she's gonna start thinking about."

A pretty waitress came by and Dave ordered a cup of coffee. She ignored him and refilled Charlie's cup. He winked at her and she smiled back. The waitress took her pot of coffee to the next table.

"So, what's she gonna start thinking about, Mr. Smartguy?"

Charlie lit a cigarette. "She's gonna start thinking about how disappointed she is that the life she has is not the one she imagined for herself. When she does that, she's gonna freeze up like a popsicle."

"I don't believe it," Dave said, trying to convince himself.

"It's true. It happened to me twice." Charlie held up two fingers for emphasis.

"I don't know, Charlie. I just don't think she's like that."

"Think about it, Dave. She's young. She still lives in the dorm, for God's sake. She sweet but she's naïve. It's not going to take much to burst her bubble."

Dave sat for a minute, thinking about what Charlie was saying.

"Let's just say for a minute that you're right. What do you think I can do to keep this from happening? I mean, I really love this girl and I don't want stupid stuff like bills and everyday worries coming between us. I don't want our sex life to fizzle out so early into our relationship."

Charlie smiled and leaned over conspiratorially.

"Well, let me just say this. The longest relationships I've ever had were with girls who were absolutely wild. Real party girls.

They were too interested in fucking to let the little stuff bother them."

Dave shook his head. "But Julie's not like that. She's a good girl. She goes to Sunday school. She's not wild."

Charlie grinned. "That can always be fixed. Most wild girls don't start out being wild. The same thing goes for sluts. They don't start out that way. It just happens through a course of events. They get a taste. Do you understand what I'm saying?" Charlie looked at Dave intently.

"I think I understand what you're getting at."

"Yes, they get a taste of what they've been missing and you can't hold them back. I mean, a drunk can't be a drunk until he tastes alcohol. The same thing goes for a slut; she can't be a slut until she gets turned out. And then, watch out, she is not going to be able to live without it."

"So, you're saying that the only way to keep Julie from going frigid is to turn her out?" Dave asked, a little bit incredulously.

"Yep. She has to become a slut."

Dave thought about reaching across the table and punching Charlie out. He really wanted to. He couldn't bear for anybody, even Charlie, to talk that way about Julie. She was so nice and so pretty. He could hardly bear it. The only thing that kept him from hitting him was the fact that Charlie usually knew what he was talking about when it came to women. He had been married twice and he was only in his mid-twenties. He had had relationships galore, but he wasn't bad at them or even bad at picking women, it was just that he was too good. It was just too easy. He got bored and couldn't help himself. The women loved him too, and that didn't help matters. He was tall, muscular and had a reputation for being a great lover. So, as a result, Dave continued to listen, even though he had his fists clenched.

"You've got to turn that girl out, Dave. I know it may be a little hard on you at first, but believe me, it'll be worth it. It'll be like heaven on earth for you after that. This girl will be insatiable. She won't be able to do anything without getting wet. It'll be so good that *you'll* be begging *her* not to have sex."

Charlie put his cigarette out and took another sip of coffee.

Dave couldn't take it anymore. He looked at Charlie, smugly sitting there, saying all that nasty stuff about his precious little Julie.

"I really don't appreciate you being so crude about Julie. She's a good girl. You don't even have the right to even say her name."

With that he got up abruptly and walked off

"I'm just trying to help you!" Charlie yelled at him as he walked out the door.

Dave got into his car and drove away from the diner. He couldn't believe that Charlie was actually saying this stuff. The nerve. He should've belted him one. Still though, he couldn't help but have a nagging feeling about the whole thing. He had been in long-term relationships before and what Charlie said had been true more often than not. After the newness wears off, things cool off considerably. Pretty soon, you might as well be brother and sister. He reminded himself that this was Julie that he was talking about. Sweet Julie. Surely, she wouldn't be this way. Surely.

Dave drove a little bit further and realized that the more he thought about it, the more doubt crept into his mind. What if Charlie was right? He didn't want to spend his married life as a celibate. Wasn't their sex life supposed to get better after they were married? He decided that Charlie was probably full of bullshit. But then again, what if he wasn't? He didn't know if he could handle being in a sexless marriage. He didn't ever want to face the thought of cheating on Julie. He didn't ever want to be forced into that situation. After about a half hour of driving around, he simply couldn't take it anymore. He picked up his cellphone.

"Okay, what can I do?"

He could tell Charlie smiled.

"Well, you don't do anything except sit back and..."

4

Julie sighed as she turned her car off. She didn't feel like working today. As she unbuckled her seatbelt, she gazed over at the mall. It seemed so far away, especially when she thought about the long walk from the parking lot. Once she left her car, she knew that the walk would seem all too short. She normally loved her job at the accessories shop, but for some reason, she just didn't feel like going in today. Maybe it was because she couldn't get her head out of the clouds now that she was engaged. She had waited so long for Dave to ask her and now he had. That had only been two weeks ago. Maybe that's what it was.

No, that wasn't true. She knew full well why she didn't want to go today. It was that guy, Charlie, the new security guard. He had started yesterday and she had been in a tither ever since. She just couldn't get him out of her mind. She just couldn't wait to get back to work so she could see him. She tingled with anticipation because she knew what awaited her when she was finally able to see him again. She had always been such a good girl, but she couldn't help but get all wet thinking about him.

She tried to compose herself and push those thoughts out of her head. She couldn't believe how she was acting now. And it was all because of Charlie's big dick. She just couldn't wait to have it inside her again. She couldn't wait to get another taste. She couldn't help but start salivating at the thought of sucking him off again.

It had started on his first day. Julie had just pulled up the metal gate to the store when she looked around and saw him standing there, checking her out. She had worn a short skirt and high heels that day. This wasn't lost on Charlie. He could definitely understand what Dave saw in her. She was a real piece. She had the kind of body that you could barely keep from jumping on. He was going to have a hard time keeping his cool with this one. Watching her bend over had almost made him start drooling. Turning this girl out was going to be a real treat.

"Nice ass," he said.

She turned around, fast. She was startled to see him standing there, leering at her. His large erection was not concealed by his polyester uniform pants. While slightly disgusted, she couldn't help but be a little intrigued by its size. She had never seen one that big before. She didn't even know they could come so big. She tried her best not to stare. She stood up and pushed her skirt down.

"I would appreciate it if you kept your comments to yourself," Julie said, quite indignantly. She looked away from him, but couldn't help but notice what a good looking guy he was. He was tall, sandy haired, muscular. Guys who looked like him weren't supposed to be perverts.

"Oh, I'm sorry," he said and smiled. "I meant it as a compliment."

She rolled her eyes, but he continued on, undaunted.

He held out his hand, "I'm Charlie. I'm the new security guard."

She hesitated at first, but she took his hand and shook it lightly, trying her best to avoid his erection. "I'm Julie. I work here."

"Oh, I know. I've heard all about you."

She looked at him a little askance. Just who was this guy?

"And what exactly have you heard?" she asked,

Charlie smoothly corrected himself. He couldn't let Julie know that it was Dave had been the one who had told him about her. He had gone through a lot of trouble to set this up just to let something as small as a slip of the tongue mess things up for him. The hardest part was working this job. He hated work in general, but, in his opinion, working as a security guard was the worst. However, it had been a necessary evil, and as he suspected, he didn't have any trouble in securing the job. They hired him, sight unseen, over the telephone. All he had to do now was put up with all the disrespect from the kids and everybody else at the mall as well, for that matter. But he could let it slide though in order to complete his mission. Besides, he realized that the job had a high shakedown potential. The kids and old people would probably be pretty easy to intimidate. He would probably never have to pay for his own lunch again.

He grinned. "Oh, I've heard a lot of things."

"Like what?" she asked, suspiciously

"I've heard that you're a very nice girl." This was true. Dave had told him that many times.

"Thank you," she said, a little relieved.

"I'm sorry, I scared you a little early, it's just that you're so hot, I just couldn't help myself."

"Oh, that's okay," Julie had always been a little on the naïve side and had never really had much experience in life. She was already twenty-one years old and Dave was the only boyfriend she had ever had. And now he was her fiancé. He wasn't very exciting, but he was exciting enough for her. At least that's what she always told herself whenever her mind started wandering towards thoughts of movie stars and other boys. But the truth be known was that she was never really interested in any kind of out-of-the-ordinary sexual activities. She just had never really been intrigued by all that stuff that she saw on the cover of Cosmopolitan. It just seemed so unnecessary for two people in love to do those kinds of things. It also seemed kind of...*perverted*.

But still...she just couldn't keep her eyes off his erection. It was just so...interesting and...delicious looking.

"How about to make it up to you, I'll go get us some coffee?" Charlie said.

Julie thought for a minute before she committed.

"I'm engaged."

"It's only coffee," Charlie smiled mischievously.

"Well, alright," Julie sighed. "After all, it's only coffee."

"I'll be back in a minute," Charlie said.

Julie went into the store and settled down to work. He seemed like a nice guy, but his hard-on was still as noticeable as it was when it was when he was creeping her out. Oh, well, she thought to herself, that's just the way boys are. Dave had told her that he sometimes got hard-ons when he was sleepy. That was probably it. Charlie was sleepy. That's why he wanted the coffee. It all made sense to her now. In a couple of minutes, Charlie came back.

"I've got the coffee, as promised," he said.

"I see."

As she sat in her car and thought about it now, it wasn't coffee that he was interested in. It was her. That's why he still had that erection!

They went into the back office and sat around for a few minutes talking about the weather and what not when Charlie had made his move. He started by distracting her with compliments, when all of a sudden, he had his hand all the way up her skirt and was yanking down her panties!

"Charlie! What do you think you're doing?"

He just kept smiling.

"You know you're interested in me. I saw you looking at my erection."

Julie blushed. He had caught her. How could she help herself? She had only seen Dave's penis and was interested to know what others looked like. There was nothing wrong with that, right?

"Julie, I know you want this. I can tell."

She blushed again. Deep down, she knew he was right, she did want this. His hand up her skirt had made her wet. She could feel her juices dripping down her leg. She got so wet when she was horny. But what was she thinking? She couldn't do this! What about Dave? He would be so hurt. She couldn't do this to him. This was so unlike her. She was a good girl. She didn't just have sex with just anybody. But then again, she had never been in this situation before.

But then he said the words that made it all seem right. Of course, she was so turned on that he could have said anything.

"It's okay. I won't tell anybody."

With that, she launched herself at him. She hungrily kissed his face and felt his erection. It was enormous! It had to be at least ten inches! He couldn't pull his pants down fast enough for her. She stuffed his cock in her mouth and started sucking it like it was some rare delicacy. She just couldn't believe how much she wanted it. She had never been like this with Dave. All thoughts of Dave were gone. Dave? Dave who? She was living for the here and now. It was like a switch had been turned on. She was doing things she had never even imagined doing. She just did what came naturally, acting on every lustful impulse. She felt like a little slut and it felt nice.

While Julie sucked his cock, Charlie reached around and rubbed her pussy. It was so wet, his fingers easily slid in. He could get three fingers in as easily as he could one. He alternated between her pussy and asshole and was surprised at how loose she was. He wondered if ol' Dave had been reaming her out and not telling him. He knew that he hadn't. She was just a natural born slut. He was surprised at easy it had been. He knew this one would be no trouble at all. This was also going to a lot of fun. She squeezed his balls as she sucked and he couldn't help but smile.

"I want you to cum in my mouth," she gasped.

"Not yet," he said. "You've got to let me fuck you first."

She stood and bent over the desk, with her back facing him. She pushed her ass towards him, beckoning him to stick his stiff penis into her wet hole. His first thrust was hard and it pressed her down onto the desk. Her breasts were squashed down so much, she could almost kiss them. He rammed her for a few minutes, and she could feel an orgasm welling inside her. It was going to come fast and it was going to come hard. She grabbed the desk as hard as she could while she bucked against him. She came hard as he pumped her.

"Fuck me!" she yelled as he thrusted.

In a matter of seconds, she emitted an almost primal grunt and started panting like a dog. She ground into him hard as she climaxed and he had a hard time holding it. He had to wait. He didn't want to cum like this.

After she was done, he pulled out and she willingly got on her knees.

"Now, I'm gonna cum in your mouth."

She grabbed his penis and started sucking it and stroking it with her fingers. She positioned herself so she would take the full brunt of his ejaculation. She didn't want to miss a single drop. He put his finger into her mouth, opening it a little wider. She held it open for him as he squirted into it. She made sure that she took the whole load in her mouth. He just tasted so good. She had always loved the taste of Dave's cum and was surprised that Charlie's could taste so much better. She was absolutely elated.

After they were through, they sat on the desk, looking at each other. Charlie looked like the cat that ate the canary and Julie looked like she was miserable. Reality had set in. She had actually started thinking about Dave and was feeling guilty. She just couldn't believe what she had just done and she couldn't believe she could be so selfish. She couldn't let this happen again.

"You've got to leave," she said.

"You sure you don't want to go again?" he said, taking a sip of his coffee. He sensed that she would flip out and tell him to leave and that she never wanted to see him again and all that, but he was confident that her resolve would not last long.

"No, you've got to get out of here."

But then they heard the sound of someone moving about the store though the paper thin walls of the office. Lucy, the assistant manager had arrived.

"It's Lucy! You've got to get out of here!"

She hurriedly put her clothes back on. Charlie dressed himself at a leisurely pace. "Hurry!" she whispered. "She'll be back here any minute!"

Sure enough, the second Charlie buttoned his last button, the office door burst open.

"Hello, Julie," she said, a little startled, "Who's this?"

"Oh, I'm Charlie," he said, casually. "I'm the new security guard. I was just showing your boss a few things back here that she needs to know about."

Julie cleared her throat, uncomfortably.

"Yes, Lucy," she said nervously. "He was just showing me a few things."

She surveyed Julie's rumpled clothes and flushed face. She also noticed Charlie's leering smile. Besides, it was kind of hard to miss the smell of sex in the air. She smiled.

"Oh," Lucy said. "I understand. I think."

"If you want, I can show you a few things, too." Charlie leered. He eyed her black hair and gorgeous body.

"Oh, no," Julie said hurriedly. "She doesn't need to know anything."

"Who says?" Lucy said a little indignantly, noticing the imprint of Charlie's sizable cock through his polyester pants.

"Yeah, you shouldn't try to keep this information to yourself, Julie," Charlie said.

Back in the car, Julie sighed. She might as well get to it. She didn't want to be late.

Julie locked her car door and got out. Yep, she dreaded going to work, but still she felt a little anticipation as she approached the mall. Sure, she had said never again, but the more she thought about it, the more she realized that she really wanted this. She was an adult and she deserved to have what she wanted. Besides, what Dave didn't know wouldn't hurt him. She came up with a million different excuses, to justify what she knew she was going to do.

5

After Charlie went home that night, he chuckled at his good fortune. He couldn't believe that his good buddy, Dave, was simply handing over his girlfriend to him to do with as he wished. He pinched himself just to see if he was awake.

As he settled into his easy chair to watch a little porn and eat a TV dinner, he was still amazed. Sure, he had women all the time, in fact he had one coming over that night, but this was a whole new dynamic. He had never experienced turning out another man's woman. He was sure that it was no different than turning out any other woman, but this time he felt he had sort of a responsibility to Dave in an odd sort of way. He really had to turn Julie out good. He had to make her into the ultimate slut. He had to turn her out so completely that she would get wet at the drop of a hat. He had to get her so she would masturbate at the mere suggestion of anything sexual in nature. He had to get her to the point where her sex drive was her prime motivator. He started to get a hard-on just thinking about it.

That Julie was something else, indeed.

He finished eating his TV dinner and took a shower, all the while thinking about his plans for Julie. He found himself with a perpetual hard-on while he went about his routine. He didn't jerk off though, because he wanted to save it for his date that night. He figured that the best approach for Julie was to go as hardcore as possible due to her inexperience. Some people might think that baby steps would be the best route, but he figured that a full out attack would be best. She would have nothing to judge her experiences against so she would think that all out extreme gangbanging, cum-slurping sex would be the norm for everybody. Of course, she would want to fit in and be just like everybody so she would accept and love whatever "adventure" he was able to create for her.

He had turned out girls before, especially back during his military days. Wherever he was stationed, he had always had a pick of willing, beautiful girls who loved a man in uniform and were looking for a way out of whatever drab, boring town they lived in. He didn't necessarily prey upon these girls' desperation, but rather just let nature take its course. He never felt like he was using them. He knew from personal experience that girls can be a hell of a lot dirtier than guys and most of the time they're just looking for an excuse to show it. He would take these girls out, and more often than not, it was them who suggested all sorts of extreme sexual activity. In fact, he had only been with a handful of women before he had gone into the service and barely knew which end was up. In a sense, it was they who turned him out at first and introduced him to the world of recreational sex. Or more specifically, it was one woman who had, effectively, been the one who had turned him out.

It had happened when he had been staying at a hotel in Texas. He had gone to the hotel bar and immediately noticed a hot older blonde woman sitting by herself at the bar. Naturally, he walked over to her. They chitchatted for a little bit and it became obvious to him what she was looking for. It wasn't long before she suggested that they go up to her room. He readily agreed. But before they could go up, she said there was something he needed to know. She told him that she was married and that her husband wanted to watch the two of them have sex. Of course, Charlie was a little put off at first because he was so young and naïve, but she was so damned good looking and he was so horny that he couldn't say no. He never even knew her name because they never achieved that level of a relationship. In his mind, he always referred to her as "the Woman." The Woman was in her early thirties, about ten years older than him at the time. She had big breasts and a tanned tight body. She smiled a lot and flashed him every time she changed positions on her barstool. No matter how uncomfortable the situation might get, how could he say no to something like that?

After they went up to her hotel room, the husband quickly brought out the liquor and poured everyone a drink.

"This is just to get everyone loosened up," he said nervously. The hard-on in his pants bulged with anticipation. Charlie looked away from it.

"Thanks," Charlie said hesitantly as he took the drink, wondering if the husband had possibly poisoned the drink. How was he to know that these people weren't going to steal a kidney or something? He tried to relax though and decided to face the inevitable.

"Drink up, honeybunch," the Woman said and winked. She tossed her head back. Something that looked that good couldn't possibly be bad, Charlie decided. He drank his drink fast, which was a good thing, because the Woman was all over him. She had her hand on his crotch and was rubbing it while playing with herself. She had her short skirt pulled up and the absence of panties allowed him easy access. The husband just sat in a chair opposite of them and watched her with rapt attention.

She pulled Charlie's cock out of his pants and started sucking on it immediately. He was already hard and her technique was impeccable. She focused on the head, in just the right spot. The pre-cum came up fast and he had to struggle not to go all the way. She was just damned good, he could hardly control himself.

"That is one massive cock you've got there," she said as she came up for air.

Charlie smiled his thanks and continued to concentrate on not coming. The Woman was good. She definitely knew her way around a dick. That was for damned sure.

The husband got a camera and started snapping pics of the two of them.

"You don't mind if I take some pics, do you?" he asked after the fact.

Did he?

"We like to have souvenirs," he laughed nervously.

Charlie again couldn't help but notice the large protrusion poking out in front of the guy's pants. There was definitely more to this picture taking than just souvenirs.

"Sure, go ahead," Charlie said. At that point he would've agreed to having his right arm amputated just to keep the Woman's mouth on his dick. Up and down, up and down. She licked and sucked the tip like a pro. How Charlie kept from blowing his wad down the back of her throat, he still didn't know. She was enthusiastic, too. It was like she was hungry for cock.

"Let's do something else," she grinned.

"Okay," Charlie said.

With that, she removed all her clothes except for her shoes. Her dress fell down around her feet. She stepped out of the dress and moved in close to Charlie, turning her back to him and rubbing her ass against his dick.

"Take off your clothes, we're gonna fuck," she said breathily.

Charlie obeyed and soon he was doing her doggie-style against the dresser. She was like a wild woman. He couldn't put it to her hard enough. She reached back and slapped him on the ass whenever he would let up.

"Fuck her good! She needs a good fucking!" the husband cheered as he snapped pics, his hard-on bulging through his pants.

They did it like that for a while but soon got on the bed.

Next, they tried missionary. He eagerly sucked on her breasts and neck. He really gave her a good fucking and she thrust against him hard, as well. He kept having to move her back down on the bed so she wouldn't bump her head into the headboard. After a couple of orgasms like this, she wanted to go back to the doggie. It was about at this time, when she relinquished control and let him take over. She wanted him to be the boss. She had just let him know what she wanted first, but now she was ready for him to take over. He readily took command. He flipped her over on her stomach and really gave it to her.

"Make her eat that bed!" the husband cried as Charlie pushed her down into the mattress. He was in charge now and he was going to fuck her like she had never fucked her before. The sweat was dripping off the both of them as he pounded her. He wasn't sure how many orgasms she had had, but with each one, he kept vowing that he was not going to cum until she had another. The husband was climbing the walls at this point and when the Woman finally erupted with a scream in her biggest orgasm yet, her wriggling and squirming and bucking were all Charlie could take. He stroked her as hard he could, cumming inside her tight pussy. He felt like he came a quart and with the large amount of semen that was oozing out of her. It certainly appeared that way. He got another hard-on instantaneously when she scooped up his cum from her pussy and swallowed it.

Yep, that was the day that Charlie had been turned out and he still thought fondly of it. He wished he knew the Woman's name so he could thank her for all that she had done for him.

Charlie put on his shoes just in time to hear the doorbell ring. He got up and answered it.

"Hi, Charlie, you ready to party?"

Charlie put his arm around the beautiful girl's waist.

"You know I am, Lucy. Just let me get my coat."

"Don't forget the lube!" Lucy.

Charlie chuckled to himself as he went to his closet. This thing was going to work out beautifully.

6

Julie was excited when she arrived at her dorm after work. She was all a flutter with thoughts about Charlie and so wet that she couldn't stand it. She couldn't keep her hands off her pussy. She constantly found herself rubbing it through her pants. She came several times, but had to eventually make herself stop. She had to get focused for her night class, but she was so horny that she knew she would not be able to concentrate much. It was *Library Science and You 403*. Her favorite. She had always looked forward to this class, so she couldn't believe that she was almost considering skipping it to stay home and masturbate. She was horrified at this thought and felt a little guilty. What was happening to her priorities? She had never intentionally skipped a class and had only missed one day of school in her life and that was because she had the flu. She only had to miss one day because she had conveniently come down with it on a Friday. She only had to miss Monday. She had been lucky, she thought.

No, she couldn't miss class. She was just going to have to get herself straightened out. She could wait until class was over to masturbate.

She stripped down to her panties and stretched out on her bed to take a short nap before class. Maybe a little sleep would take her mind off that thug, Charlie. Knowing her luck, she knew that she would probably just end up dreaming about him. She soon fell fast asleep, but, inevitably just as she had predicted, she immediately started a sex dream about him. She couldn't escape that big cock of his even in her slumber. Since she had always been avid reader of her mother's romance novels, her dream was typically something that could have easily been taken from one of them. In it, Charlie was a pirate and she was passenger on a ship that he and his crew had boarded. The other passengers cowered with fear as the pirates robbed them, one by one. Julie and the other women nervously waited for the ravishing they would no doubt receive at the hands of these brutes. They would probably be abducted and forced into prostitution by the sailors. This thought made Julie a little queasy, but also a little horny. Being the ship's whore had always been a secret fantasy of hers. But that was just a fantasy. This was the real thing and she was scared. The dirty buccaneers lasciviously leered at the females and ripped their clothes off and began feeling them up. Naturally, Cap'n Charlie oversaw the raid and as he surveyed the spoils he was immediately drawn to her. He walked over to her with the intensity of a pervert and cut off her blouse with his cutlass. He licked his lips with anticipation.

"Leave me alone!" she screamed.

"ARRRRR!!!!" Charlie yelled and whipped out his erect cock. He grinned like a madman. "Pull up your skirts and prepare to be boarded!"

He lunged for her and she dodged out of his way. While she was frightened, she couldn't help but be intrigued by the size of his member. She tried to run away, but he pulled her back. She managed to escape his grasp again, climbing up and up, towards the crow's nest. Charlie followed her, staying just a few steps behind. He cut off her skirt as she climbed. As she climbed up, completely nude, the air kissed her breasts and pussy. She couldn't help but start feeling aroused. She looked down and saw Charlie right behind her, cock still erect and bouncing as he climbed. Maybe getting ravished wouldn't be so bad after all. He was the captain, after all. She continued to climb. By the time she made it to the crow's nest, she was dripping. She couldn't wait for the pirate to come up and give it to her. Wielding his cock like a cutlass, Charlie climbed in and she welcomed his advances.

She had only been asleep for about five minutes when Josie came into the room. The first thing she noticed was that Julie was lying in her panties, the second thing she noticed was that the girl was playing with herself and the last thing she noticed was that she was completely asleep.

She watched her for a few seconds and immediately got turned on. Her eyes lingered on the pretty brunette's breasts as they heaved up and down with her breathing. The effect it had on her was almost hypnotic as she watched the girl sleep. She had been waiting for an opportunity like this ever since she had met Julie. She couldn't help but put her hand down into her jeans and rub herself. What little pubic hair she had was already damp from seeing pretty Julie writhing on the bed. She longed to climb into bed with the girl and lick that beautiful pussy. It was just too much for her to bear. Her mouth began to water and she could feel her breathing quicken. She wanted Julie now more than she had ever wanted her before. She moved closer to the bed and began to crawl into bed with her. But before she could get started, she paused and stopped herself.

This was wrong. She couldn't do this. She couldn't just molest Julie in her sleep. It just wouldn't be right. If she did this there would be no going back. Julie might hate her and she wouldn't be able to handle not seeing her anymore. If the girl had been awake, it would've been okay to approach her. Sure, she might be rejected, but at least Julie would have had a choice.

But still, how often did something like this happen? This was like fate or something. It was like winning the lottery.

Josie said what the hell and went for it.

She took off her clothes and crawled into the bed beside the sleeping girl. She snuggled in close behind her and put her hands on Julie's breasts. They felt so good that Josie couldn't resist kissing her neck. Julie immediately responded with a moan and turned to Josie and began hunching her leg. Josie was pleasantly startled and came immediately. This was even better than she had dreamed. She worked her right leg between Julie's so their pussies could touch. They both started hunching immediately. Josie reached down between Julie's legs and felt her dampness. She scooped up three fingers worth and with trembling fingers tasted it.

Josie came again. Julie's juice tasted as wonderful and as sweet as she imagined. She sucked on Julie's tits and was so turned on that she would've done anything she came into contact with. She couldn't tell if Julie was coming or not, but she could tell that she sure was enjoying it. Julie moaned and writhed, grinding her pussy against Josie's. Josie was worked up to a full froth by the time Julie began speeding up the pace. In her dream, Julie was getting fucked, standing up in the crow's nest. Meanwhile, down on the deck, the pirates were having an orgy with the women of the ship. She was too turned on. She just couldn't get enough of Cap'n Charlie's massive cock.

Josie came three times within a few seconds, no longer caring at all if Julie woke up. An experience like this was worth it, no matter what the consequences. After about a couple of minutes of non-stop grinding, Julie came with an explosive moan.

Then she woke up.

She started when she saw Josie lying in bed with her, lips on her breasts, legs between hers and grinding against her pussy. She started to pull away, but realized how good it felt. She was a little puzzled and little bit ashamed, but due to what Charlie had been doing to her, she found herself to be a little curious.

Josie noticed she was awake and abruptly stopped her movements. Red-faced, she quickly pulled away and got off the bed.

"I'm so sorry, Julie. I…" she stammered as she pulled her clothes on.

Julie looked at the nervous girl, a little bit dumbfounded.

"Did you just…"

Josie couldn't even look at her.

"I'll move out, if you want, Julie. I just couldn't help myself. You were there asleep, masturbating and I've had this thing for you…"

"I was masturbating? In my sleep?"

"Yes, I'm so sorry. I should've just left.

"Did you say you have a thing for me?" Julie said, finding herself getting aroused. She couldn't help but notice the delicious shape of Josie's breasts and hips.

"Yes." Josie hung her head and sat down on a chair opposite Julie. "I've wanted to kiss you for so long, I can't even remember."

Julie thought for a second. She couldn't help but be flattered. While she had never really considered being with a woman before, she found herself to be getting highly turned on by the thought of Josie kissing her and feeling her up in her sleep. She had been having the most intense sex dream she had ever had because of Josie. She just wondered how all this would feel if she was awake.

"Do you still want to kiss me?"

Josie smiled shyly.

"More than anything."

Julie got off the bed and went over to her.

"I hope you want to do more than just kiss."

Josie thought she had died and gone to heaven as Julie got down on her knees and began to eat her wet pussy. She rubbed

Julie's head as she worked her tongue. While Josie found it hard to believe that Julie hadn't ever been with a woman, Julie couldn't believe that a pussy could taste so good. The two girls quickly moved over to the bed where they kissed, ate and hunched each other until Julie had to go to class.

7

Julie's high heels clicked noisily across the mall's marble floors. She could feel eyes on her as she made her way to the accessory shop. This wasn't unusual. She usually attracted a crowd wherever she went due to how sexy she looked, especially her ass. She just couldn't help it. It actually made her feel pretty good to know that men liked to look at it. This was especially true since Charlie had gotten a hold of her. These furtive looks only helped to fuel her masturbatory fantasies. Besides, she did have a great ass. Hell, she worked out enough, she might as well get some benefit from it.

She looked around to see if Charlie was anywhere around. He wasn't. Thank God. She really needed a breather from him. It was almost like she was overdosing on him and the moral ramifications due to the *Dave Situation*. Technically, she was cheating and no matter what she told herself, she still had not found a good way to justify it. She had felt so guilty the previous night when she had gone to Dave's apartment, she was in absolute agony. She had always heard that the truth will set a person free, but she didn't dare tell him about it. Even if she assured him that it had nothing to do with their relationship and it was simply recreational fun, there was no telling what he might do. He was pretty laid back, but she didn't want to push him too much. As they had sat around talking, she couldn't help but think about Charlie's big dick up inside of her. She got wet just thinking about it and as hard as she tried, she couldn't push the thought out of her mind. When she drank the water that Dave offered her, she couldn't help but taste Charlie's semen. She had never been fucked like that before and she knew that she would have to struggle not to let it become an addiction for her. She tried her best not to give Dave any reason to suspect that something was up with her, but as he sat across from her droning on about his day, he could tell that something was up indeed. He suspected that Charlie had started the turning out process. If she had only known that his reaction was quite the opposite of what she expected, she wouldn't have given herself so much hell.

"What's wrong, honey? Did you have a bad day at work?" he said. It was obvious to him from her mussed up hair and clothes that she had been having sex. Besides he could smell it on her. She definitely had the look of the sated. He was a little surprised at how turned on he was at the thought of her doing all sorts of nasty things with Charlie. His imagination was filled with all sorts of scenarios and he couldn't wait to find out if they were correct.

"Nothing," she said guiltily. "I had a great day."

She wasn't lying either. Charlie had nailed her twice in the food court bathroom.

"That's nice," he said and went back to droning, hiding his curiosity.

As she listened, her mind wandered back to Charlie and his massive cock. She wondered how something like that would feel in her ass. She had never had anal sex before, but she figured that it would feel pretty nice. She crossed and uncrossed her legs several times. She was just getting so horny thinking about it that she just couldn't stand it. She was going to have to fuck something quick and the fact that the love of her life, Dave, was handy made it an ideal situation. When he came over to give her a kiss, she just couldn't stand it anymore. She grabbed him and before he knew what hit him, she unzipped his pants and had his cock in her mouth in seconds.

"Julie! What's going on?" he gasped. Now it was obvious that Charlie been doing something, he thought. This was definitely out of the ordinary behavior for her.

She pulled the dick out of her mouth. "Can't you see I've got my mouth full?" She went back to sucking. As she sucked she massaged her pussy, using the juice to lubricate her asshole. She was so wet and ready that her fingers easily slipped in. When she started tasting pre-cum, she put it down. "You can cum in my mouth after you fuck me in the ass."

Julie couldn't believe what had just come out of her mouth. She sounded just like some kind of slut or something. Dave, however, didn't seem to mind a bit. In fact he just started grinning like some kind of oaf.

"You don't know how long I've wanted to do that!"

With that, he shoved it in, slowly, right up to the balls. Julie screamed with delight as he worked it in. It hurt a little at first, but when he got fully in and started pumping, she immediately had an orgasm. She bucked up against him hard and rubbed her clit.

"Fuck me," she whined. She just couldn't get enough. She panted as he pumped her. She had another orgasm a couple of minutes later. Her juice was dripping down her legs.

She then got down on her knees and started sucking off Dave, who, almost on cue, came all over her face. She lapped his semen up like a dog. Dave just stood there, smiling the biggest, happiest smile she had ever seen. She smiled back as she swallowed, but still couldn't help but feel the slightest touch of guilt because of the origins of her lust.

Even though they cuddled afterward, she still felt a little bit slutty. However, because it was the best sex they had ever had, she tried to not let it bother her. And it wasn't because of what had happened with Dave, but because she knew what would happen if she saw Charlie. Her resolve would never be enough with a cock like his. She was now just a slut for cock, any cock and she would just have to accept it.

All this was definitely changing her reasons for working at the mall.

When Julie arrived at the store, she was a little surprised to see that Lucy was already there, behind the counter, standing by the cash register.

"Hello, Lucy, you're here early."

Lucy was a little startled.

"Oh, hello, Julie." Lucy quickly closed the cash register drawer. She was still a little wrung out from being with Charlie the night before. He had fucked her every possible way that she knew to fuck and then a little bit more. If she didn't know better, she could've sworn that she was walking bowlegged. Charlie had told her all about his plan for Julie and had asked if she would like to help. Charlie said he needed her to seduce Julie and also to get him some money from the cash register. He said that he needed plenty of cash if he was going to turn the girl out. What he needed the money for, he wasn't very clear, but Lucy had no reason to doubt that turning out a girl required money. Even though when she had been turned out, she had been wined and dined with Taco Bell and Budweiser.

At first Lucy was a little reluctant to help, but then Charlie said that he wouldn't have sex with her anymore if she didn't. That was the clincher. Besides, she had always thought while Julie was a very pretty girl, she was also very stuck up. She couldn't wait to see her all slutted out.

Julie walked over behind the counter.

"Wha'cha doing?"

"Oh, nothing, Julie, nothing at all," she stammered. "Just making sure we've got plenty of money." She hurriedly shut the register drawer.

"That's nice," Julie said. She stared at Lucy for a minute and realized that she had never noticed just how pretty Lucy was. She had dark hair and an olive complexion. Her breasts were perfectly proportioned to her hips and her thin waist was just oh so alluring. She could see why Lucy was so popular with the boys. Being with Josie had really done something for her. She was beginning to see women in a whole new light.

Lucy noticed that Julie was staring at her and couldn't help but smile. Maybe this was going to easier than she had thought.

"You're checking me out, aren't you?"

Now, it was Julie's time to stammer.

"N-no…"

Lucy smiled and moved a little closer to Julie.

"It's okay. I get checked out by girls all the time. In fact, I like it."

Julie pulled away slightly, just out of habit. This whole bisexuality thing was still a little new.

"That's nice," she said uncomfortably.

"Don't be scared, Julie. Don't tell me that you've never been attracted to a girl."

"I'm afraid, I haven't, Lucy," she lied out of habit.

Lucy looked her solidly in the eyes, slightly smirking.

That little bitch, Julie thought. She knows I'm lying. Lucy moved in closer and put her hand behind Julie's waist, sensuously rubbing the small of her back. Before Julie knew what was going on, Lucy pulled her to her and gave her a deep kiss. At first, Julie wanted to pull back just to try to back up her lie, but the kiss was just so good she just went with it.

Julie looked around to see if anybody was watching. Nobody was. Good.

"Let's get down behind the counter," Lucy said, breathlessly.

The ruse was over. Julie might as well follow what her body dictated and obey the wetness that was already forming in her pussy. She knew she wouldn't feel any guilt over this. Having sex with a girl wasn't cheating, it was just fun. It was a whole different ballgame in her mind.

Lucy almost purred her agreement. She already had a hand on her clit.

Once down on the floor, Lucy had Julie's skirt up and her panties off in seconds flat. She was definitely an old pro at this. She rubbed Julie's pussy while kissing her mouth. Julie pulled her own shirt up so Lucy could have access to her full breasts. This just felt so good, that she could barely handle it. And when Lucy started licking her pussy she knew she was going to cum. Lucy fingerfucked her while sucking her clit and Julie came fast. Lucy kissed her and she could taste herself on the girl's lips. The girl taste was so good that she just had to give Lucy a try. She wondered if she tasted any better than Josie. She laid Lucy back and put her head up under Lucy's skirt. She was delighted to find that the dark haired girl wasn't wearing panties. She eagerly put her mouth on Lucy's clit and went to town. Lucy tasted every bit as good as Josie. Like semen, this was a taste that she knew that she was not going to be able to live without.

After Lucy had orgasmed twice, they both got up, kissing and giggling

"Are you sure, you've never done that before?" Lucy grinned.

Julie smiled shyly.

But then, before she could answer, something happened that wiped the smile right off her face. It was Charlie. He was standing right in front of the counter.

"I hope you saved some for me," he said and winked at Lucy.

She smiled and winked back.

Julie couldn't help but blush. He had been there the whole time! She couldn't do anything without him sneaking around.

Sensing her discomfort, Charlie laughed.

"I'll be back around later, when I've got a little more time." He turned and walked out.

"Oooh…it's that security guy that was here yesterday," Lucy said. "He's so hot. I bet he's got a big dick." She looked at Julie to try to gauge her reaction to her comments.

Julie didn't say anything but got a far away look in her eyes, thinking about what Charlie had in store for her. Lucy knew what she was thinking too, but was more than a little preoccupied with figuring out a way to take some money from the store. However, her problem was solved when she took a look at the register. It was wide open and emptied. Charlie had already beaten her to it.

A couple of days later, Julie walked from her dorm to the library. She couldn't help but notice what an extremely hot day it was. She wondered if it just wasn't the weather that was making it hot. No, she knew it wasn't just the weather. It was warmer than usual, but she just wasn't hot temperature-wise, she was hot on the inside as well. As she walked, she couldn't help but feel the need for a good stiff cock up her pussy. She almost ached to be filled. She promised herself that as soon as she made it to the library she would go to the ladies room and masturbate. It was the only way that she was going to be able to make it. As she made her way, a gust of wind came up out of nowhere, blowing her skirt up, revealing her pantyless triangle. She didn't get into any hurry to push the skirt down as she looked around to see if anyone had seen her. Unfortunately for her, no one was looking. She wished that someone had seen her. Maybe, it would make them horny enough to come over and approach her for sex. She realized that this was a little naïve, but that's the way it happened in the porno movies, wasn't it? That's what her life had been like since she had met Charlie. One big porno film.

Regardless, the wind felt wonderful, blowing between her legs. That morning, she had decided to stop wearing panties, so it felt especially invigorating. This was a big step for her. She had had a little hesitation about this big step of going without underwear, but the more she had thought about it, the more natural it seemed. Besides, she had watched a show on television saying that underwear was only a relatively recent necessity and that back in the old days, it was unheard of for a woman to wear anything under her skirt. That was all it took to convince her, but of course, she was so to the point of horniness that all it would have taken for her to think it was okay was the mere suggestion that such behavior was permissible for a proper young lady. And besides, who was she to buck history?

The wind blew once more and up went her skirt again. This time, she left it up for a little while longer, allowing the world to see her pussy and ass. The thought of a stranger looking at her really turned her on and she couldn't help but touch herself a little bit as she pretended to hide her nudity. It was hard to imagine that just a little while ago, that same thought would have disgusted her. She wondered how she could have possibly thought such a thing. It seemed so silly now. In fact it seemed so silly that she almost wanted to deliberately raise her skirt somewhere where someone would definitely see her. It would be so fun to see their red faces when she "discovered" them looking at her. She hoped for the gusts of wind to continue.

As she walked, she also couldn't help but notice that she was starting to check out all the other students, both male and female. She giggled. I'm becoming a bad girl, she thought to herself. While her heart was with Dave, she couldn't help but imagine herself in various situations with everyone she encountered. In the past, when she walked past a girl, she would have thought, "nice hair." However now, she thought, "nice breasts." When it came to the guys, whenever she saw a group of them together, she couldn't help but imagine what it would be like for her to be in the center of them. Gangbanging.

But there was Dave, once again. She still felt a little guilty about what she was doing to him, but the funny thing about it was that the more she screwed around on him, the less guilty she felt. With this in mind, she resolved that the only way she was going to get over it was to fuck as much as possible. It was definitely an agreeable therapy to her.

She couldn't wait to get to the library, but not just because she couldn't wait to masturbate. As a part of her study to become a librarian, it was required that she work a few hours a week there as a sort of internship. The Library Science department called it

Lab. She jokingly called it free forced labor. Still, she loved it. She didn't really do that much and aside from the small amount of work that she did, which primarily consisted of putting books back on the shelf. She usually had plenty of time to prowl around the library, looking at books. Lately though, since Charlie had come onto the scene, she found herself going more and more to the *Human Sexuality* section. She was always trying to find new techniques to try out, especially regarding masturbation. She didn't share this info with Charlie because she didn't want him to think that he was the sole source of her sexual liberation.

Upon entering the library, she immediately went to the Head Librarian's office to check in. This was something she did every day when she went to her lab. The other students in her lab arrived around the same time as she did. They signed in and waited to receive their instructions. Julie hoped that she would get the bookstacks again. As the Head Librarian handed out the assignments to each student, Julie noticed something that had escaped her on all her previous times she had been in the office. It was a sculpture that sat unobtrusively on the bookshelf behind the Librarian's office. In the past, Julie had always thought it was a pretty thing, but had never really understood what it was. She had thought that it must be some sort of modern art or something. However, now, she noticed something different about it. Maybe it was Charlie's influence on her, but if she wasn't mistaken, the sculpture was some sort of penis!

She looked slyly at the Librarian, a woman in her forties, to see if her new deductive powers would be able to discern anything. She certainly didn't look like the type of person who would have such a suggestive whatnot. She was a good looking older woman, her hair was up, with a deliciously tight body—she was a runner—and her clothes were slightly sexy, but conservative. She wore glasses and had never been married. In fact, no one that Julie knew had ever even heard of her dating anyone. It just didn't make sense to Julie, who was still quite green in the ways of adults.

Hmmmm, Julie thought. There's nothing really unusual about her, but then she took a closer look at the bookshelf. It was filled with books about sex! This woman was might be just like her. Sex crazy.

Congratulating herself on her powers of observation, Julie couldn't help but be elated. She was just like Sherlock Holmes she thought. It would be so good if the woman was a nympho like her. It would be nice to be able to actually talk to somebody about how much she loved sucking dick and getting fucked. She certainly couldn't talk about it to Dave.

Julie dallied around the office until after the other students had left. She simply had to talk to the Librarian. When everyone else had finally filed out of the office, she closed the door. The Librarian looked at her curiously.

"I noticed your sculpture," Julie said nervously, not really sure about how to say what she was about to say.

"Okay..." the Librarian said, beginning to smile a little bit. It was a wicked little smile because she knew that she had been found out.

"I like it. I like the shape, if you know what I mean," Julie said, uncomfortably. She felt like she wanted to sink into the floor. This was more embarrassing than she had thought it would be. Still, the cat was out of the bag now, she might as well continue.

"Uh huh. I think I might." The Librarian smiled a little more at the girl's discomfort.

"I also like your taste in books," Julie clumsily pointed to the sex books.

The Librarian continued to look at her and smile. It was obvious that she was getting a big kick out of this. Sure it was a little cruel, making the poor girl squirm, but that didn't make it any less entertaining. Besides, if this girl wanted to find out something personal like this, she was going to have to work for it.

At this Julie panicked. Maybe she was wrong. Maybe it was just a coincidence that the Librarian had a phallus and bunch of sex books in her office. Maybe they meant absolutely nothing. Maybe they weren't even her books. Maybe she had just made a complete fool out of herself. She would never be able to return to the library again.

"I'm sorry," she blurted and started to run out of the office. However, before she had a chance to take more than a couple of steps, the Librarian stopped her.

"Relax, Julie. It's okay. I'm not offended. In fact, I'm flattered that you noticed. Most people have no clue as to what this stuff is."

Julie slumped with relief and embarrassment.

"I...I think I read too much into it. I hope I didn't..."

But before she could get any further, the Librarian interrupted her.

"Here's my address," she said as she scribbled onto a post-it note. "I'm having a little party tonight. From your interest in my books and sculpture, I think you might enjoy it. Be there at nine tonight."

Julie looked at her hesitantly.

"Can I bring a friend?"

The Librarian thought about it for a minute and smiled.

"No, come alone. You can bring someone the next time."

That night, Julie was nervous as hell. She wasn't really sure what kind of party it was, but she was pretty sure that it wasn't like any of the ice cream socials or Library Science parties that she had attended in the past. She didn't tell Josie the details of the party, just that she was going out. Dave had been a little harder to get around. She had had to tell him a white lie and say that she had to help the Librarian with a few things that night for extra credit. Technically, it was all true, except for the extra credit part.

Josie was especially curious for some reason. Julie noticed that the girl had a little crush on her ever since they had gotten together. It was nothing really overt, but it was there nonetheless. Julie was very flattered, but wanted to keep her options open. Her main concern was that that she didn't want to hurt Josie's feelings. Fortunately, for her though, Josie didn't seem have a problem with this so things hadn't gotten sticky. Besides, Josie tramped around all the time. While, she wasn't as active as Julie, she was always going out clubbing and staying out with whatever guy or girl she happened to pick up. Julie thought, perhaps, that she should make it clear that they were in no way monogamous. She also realized that it was possible that Josie just looked at their time together as somewhat special. Maybe that was it. Julie didn't know. However, the one thing she did know was that Josie sure knew how to eat a pussy.

"So, what kind of party is it?" Josie asked as she helped brush Julie's hair.

"Oh, it's just a library thing," Julie said evasively. "Just a bunch of us boring library types, getting together and talking about the Dewey Decimal system."

"God, how boring," Josie said.

"Yeah, Lucy at work said the same thing," Julie said. Actually, she hadn't said anything about it all to Lucy or Charlie either, for that matter. She didn't want them knowing everything about her. She did have to keep some things separate.

After she got ready, she took a good look at herself in the mirror.

Josie whistled and came over and ran her index finger down Julie's leg, tracing the outline of her side and hips, starting at her rib cage. Julie was instantly turned on, and if it hadn't been such a bitch getting into the dress, she would have been tempted to take it off.

"You are so hot!" Josie said.

Julie stared at the reflection looking back at her and had to agree. She was absolutely dressed to kill. She wore a tight little black dress and six-inch heels. It was a simple outfit, but extremely sexy and classy. Of course, she didn't wear any panties. Julie just hoped she wasn't overdressed for the party.

Before she could think about it, Josie had her hands around Julie and was kissing her. Julie didn't resist and after a brief feel-up, the girls finally broke apart.

"I'm sorry, I just couldn't resist," Josie said, breathlessly.

"That's okay. I love it when you do that."

Josie helped her smooth her dress. "I hope I didn't wrinkle you."

"Don't worry about it. It'll probably get wrinkled in the car anyway."

The two girls kissed again before Julie left for the party.

It was about ten minutes after nine when Julie arrived at the house. It was situated in a middle class suburb about two exits up the interstate. The neighborhood was nice and well kept and Julie couldn't help but notice that the Librarian had the most isolated house on the block. It had the biggest lot and was well surrounded by a large security fence and lots of trees. The driveway and street in front of the house were filled with cars. Most were new and fairly expensive.

Julie parked down a little side street and prayed that she wouldn't get towed, but figured that they would have to tow everyone else, too, so she didn't worry about it too much.

After walking the short distance to the Librarian's house, she hesitantly rang the doorbell. She could hear the sounds of people laughing and music playing coming from within the house. Apparently the party was in full swing. After a few minutes, the Librarian came to the door and let her in. Julie was happy to see her, but was a little surprised at her attire, or lack of it. The Librarian was standing at the door completely nude. And from the looks of the room, so was everyone else.

"I'm so glad you could make it, Julie."

"Well, I'm glad to be here," the girl said, nervously. She couldn't help but notice what a nice body the Librarian had. Her breasts were large and perfect and her legs and ass were to die for.

"First thing though, you're going to have to lose those clothes."

"So this is a…"

The Librarian nodded her head and smiled.

So much for worry about being overdressed, Julie thought. She pulled off the dress which the Librarian gingerly took and hung up in the closet.

"No underwear…nice," the Librarian murmured.

Julie started to take off the shoes, but Librarian stopped her.

"Leave the pumps on. They look great."

Julie obeyed.

After she was fully undressed except for the shoes, the Librarian led her around the house introducing her to various people, some of whom were professors from the college. There were also a few students here and there, but most of the people were in their thirties and forties. Some were even as old as sixty or seventy, or at least it seemed that way to Julie.

"You don't find a lot of young people in the Lifestyle," the Librarian said. "I mean, there's quite a few, but mostly they're a little bit older."

Julie looked at her quizzically. *Lifestyle?*

Sensing that the girl had no idea of what she was talking about, the Librarian elaborated.

"You know, the Swinging Lifestyle?"

"Oh," Julie said, still a little befuddled. She decided not to pursue any further questions because she didn't want to sound like she didn't know what she was doing.

After introducing her to everyone in the room, the Librarian took her aside.

"Now, that you've been introduced to everyone, I'm gonna leave you on your own. I've got a few things to attend to."

Julie nodded.

After the Librarian left, a very elegant couple in their sixties approached her.

"My, what lovely breasts you have," the fellow said. Julie noticed that while he was nude, he was still wearing a cravat. It looked a little odd, but it suited him though.

His wife smiled in agreement.

"Thanks," Julie said, not really knowing what else to say.

"If you want to have a threesome, we would be more than happy to help," the wife said eagerly.

Julie nodded. While they were a good looking couple, they were still a little old for her.

She mingled around the room for a while longer, talking and laughing with people, wondering what the big deal was. There wasn't any sex going on. She had always thought that swingers were always doing it, but all these people seemed to be doing was talking and drinking. People were gathered around in the kitchen, snacking on finger food that was spread out the counter. Nope, it just didn't seem that sexual. It was just all done in the...*nude*.

But then she noticed something. There were a lot fewer people in the room than there had been a little while earlier.

Where were all the people?

Then she began to notice that some couples were walking towards one of the back bedrooms. She decided to follow them.

It was then that she finally knew what was going on and she knew where everyone was.

They were in the back bedroom having an orgy!

She looked among the writhing bodies to see any that she recognized and was only able to pick out the Librarian.

She began to juice up immediately at the smell of all the sex in the room. Not quite knowing how to approach the group, she decided to just jump in. She suddenly felt the urgent need for cock and she didn't care how she fulfilled it. She didn't have to wait long. As soon as she presented her pussy, it was quickly filled. Her breath was taken away at the rapidity of how quickly her desires were met. She came immediately. She quickly found another dick and started sucking while the dick in her pounded her silly. After another orgasm, she felt the guy squirt into her, but before she could even take a breath, another dick replaced it. In front of her, she felt hot semen fill her mouth just to be replaced, seconds later, by a hot pussy.

She continued like this for a while, just fucking and sucking until finally, she was face to face with the Librarian.

The Librarian smiled at her.

"Here, honey, I've got something I've been dying to do to you."

She grabbed Julie's legs and locked them between hers, so their pussies would touch. She Librarian smiled a wicked smile and began to hump. Julie thought that it felt simply great and eagerly followed her body's directive to hump back. They bucked and humped like that until both were spent.

After they were finished, the Librarian looked over at her.

"Don't think you're getting any special treatment at the Library."

Julie looked at her puzzledly.

The Librarian laughed.

"I'm just joking. A girl like you always gets A's in my classes," she said and winked. She rubbed her finger up Julie's leg.

They both laughed until they were ready to go at it again.

10

A few days later, as Julie got into her car to leave the mall, Charlie pulled up behind her in his truck, blocking her from leaving the parking spot.

"What do you want?" Julie said getting out of car and trying to act pissed off. She was beginning to get so conditioned to equating him with sex that she felt herself getting a little wet at the very sight of him.

"Just wondering if you want to get a bite to eat? I know a place that serves some great barbeque," Charlie said as he leaned out his window. He hoped and prayed that she would get into the car. He had come up with this scheme a couple of days earlier and couldn't wait to put it into action. All she had to do was agree to go with him to the restaurant. He had to keep things interesting if he was going to turn her out completely and he had almost been a panic because felt like he was losing control of her. He had also been at a loss because it had been a while since he had come up with something new for her to engage in...until he had thought his current plan, however.

Hmmm, Julie thought to herself. It's almost like a real date. This was a little scary for her, because she didn't really want to date Charlie. She just wanted to fuck him. She didn't want this to get icky or anything. Sure, he had a great cock, but he was a security guard. Besides, Dave was her man, not Charlie.

"I don't know. I'm meeting my boyfriend for dinner tonight."

Charlie rolled his eyes. This wasn't turning out the way he had hoped. He was losing his hold on her.

"Forget about that loser. What he doesn't know won't hurt him."

"Screw you. I'm not going to let you talk about him that way."

Charlie humbled himself a little, still leaning out of the truck window. He had to make one last stab.

"Look, I'm sorry. I didn't mean anything by it. I'm sure he's a great guy."

Julie looked at him closely. He looked sincere.

Charlie's voice grew a little softer.

"Look, how about you just come with me. I hate eating alone. If you don't want anything, I'll buy you a beer and we'll talk. We really do need to get to know each other a little better, don't you think?"

He was right, Julie thought. They did need to get to know each other a little better. After all, he had been fucking her silly on a regular basis and they had hardly even exchanged ten words. Besides, he seemed just like a little boy right now, not wanting to be alone and all. She felt a little foolish for thinking that he wanted to do more than just fuck.

"Okay," she said. "But I don't have a lot of time."

Charlie grinned. "Get in." He was almost giggling with anticipation.

They chitchatted a little bit on the way to the barbeque joint. It was way over on the black side of town, a place where Julie had never really felt that comfortable. It wasn't that she was prejudiced or anything, she just had heard that it wasn't safe for pretty white girls to go over there alone. That's why she wasn't afraid now. She had Charlie to protect her if anybody tried anything funny. Charlie was pretty talkative. He talked about the fact that he used to be in the Marines and told her a little bit about his life. It gave him a whole new depth that she had hitherto thought was nonexistent. It almost made him seem like he was more than just a stud. The more she got to know him, the better she felt about screwing him. She was feeling more and more positive that her relationship with her boyfriend was benefiting from having someone like Charlie around. Had her sex life with Dave not drastically improved because of fucking Charlie? That was a definite improvement to her relationship and there wasn't anything wrong with that.

They parked and walked into the barbeque place. There were only a couple of people there and almost all the staff knew Charlie.

"Yo, C," a big black muscular guy named Freddy said as they walked in.

"Yo, Freddy," Charlie said.

"Who's this pretty lady you've got with you?"

"This is Julie. She's the hot little piece I've been telling you out."

Julie blushed. Normally she would've gotten mad at someone for saying something like that to her, but in this case it made her feel good. She liked being a hot little piece of ass.

Freddy looked her up and down like a dog checking out a piece of meat.

"I heard that," he said smacking his lips.

Julie felt a little uncomfortable at Freddy's behavior, but couldn't help but become a little turned on.

Charlie turned to Julie and introduced Freddy.

"I eat here a lot."

"Oh," Julie said.

"Well, we're ready," Charlie said to Freddy, grinning.

Freddy smiled. "Follow me."

With that, they began to walk towards the back of the restaurant, into the kitchen area.

"Aren't we going to eat in the dining room?" Julie asked.

"No, y'all getting the VIP treatment."

"Cool," Julie said.

Charlie gave Freddy a sly look.

After being introduced to the other workers and a brief tour of the kitchen, Charlie grabbed Julie and started kissing her on the neck. They were standing at the prep table, in full view of the other workers. They were all big black guys approximately the same size as Freddy and they watched with rapt attention.

"Charlie!!!" she squealed, not resisting. "Everybody's gonna see!"

"That's the point," he murmured as he started feeling her breasts.

She had never thought about doing it in front of people, but this was oddly arousing. She was getting wetter by the instant. She loved the fact that she was finding out more and more about her sexuality.

"But what about the health inspectors?" She breathily protested as Charlie pulled down her skirt.

"Fuck the health inspectors," Freddy said, pulling out his dick and stroking it.

Julie was a little surprised at the bold gesture, but she couldn't take her eyes off the thing. It was huge! She had thought Charlie's dick was big, but this guy was hung like a horse. She looked around and all the other workers were also masturbating. They were well-endowed as well. She was a little shocked at herself as she found herself salivating at the sight of their cocks.

Charlie turned her around so her back was facing him and rubbed her pussy. She was so horny his fingers easily slipped inside of her. He slapped her ass as she writhed on his fingers.

He leaned over to her, "I want you to suck Freddy's dick."

She hesitated for a second so she wouldn't like too much of a slut, but in reality, she couldn't wait to get her lips around that big black rod.

It was so big she could barely get her lips around it, but she sucked it hard while Charlie started banging her doggie-style. All the other guys gathered around her stroking their dicks. Julie knew that this was going to be a gangbang and she couldn't wait. She couldn't believe she was thinking like this. She had never even imagined such a thing before she had met Charlie, but here she was in the middle of one. She wanted this so badly, she was aching for it. She knew she was not going to be happy until she had tasted the cum of every single man in the room.

And so it began, she would suck one and the next one would fuck her. She couldn't believe she was this insatiable. She had always had a problem with Dave coming before she did, but in this situation there was no danger of that. She could come as much as she wanted, and she would have a new guy to pump away.

When the third guy stuck it in, she found herself face first in a plate of ribs on the prep table. At first she tried to move them away, but Freddy put them back in her face.

"Eat them ribs, girl. Fuck him and eat the ribs."

"Sure, why not?" she said and picked up a rib.

"Like 'em?" he asked.

She licked one of her fingers and said, "Almost as much as your cock."

At this, he rammed her a little harder, but she didn't let go of the plate. So she ate ribs, while each man took turns giving it to her.

After they had all had a turn (and she had finished the ribs), Charlie laid her on the cold steel table and they started again. She had a dick in each hand, one in her mouth and one in her pussy. The only place she didn't have one was her ass, but that was remedied quickly.

"Let's fill up all three holes!" Charlie said.

Freddy started to move her into position for the double penetration, but Charlie stopped.

"No, man. You can have the pussy, but that ass is mine."

Julie squirmed with anticipation as she waited for him to stick his dick in her ass.

"Fuck my ass!"

After everybody got into position and started moving, she had the biggest orgasm she had ever had in her life. All the black hands on her white body and the black dicks fucking the hell out of her were just too much to take.

"Fuck me, Goddamnit!" she screamed.

When one of the workers pulled out and was getting ready to cum, Charlie stopped him.

"We're gonna do a bukkake on this girl."

Julie didn't know what a bukkake was, but she was sure she would like it.

Charlie motioned her to get down on her knees on the floor. When she was in position, all the guys got around her and they all exploded all over her face. She couldn't lick up the cum fast enough. She had to wipe it up with her hands and put it in her mouth. She didn't want to lose a drop.

"Yeah, lick it all up, baby," Freddy coaxed. He took his finger and opened her mouth, scooping the cum up with his fingers and placing it into her mouth. She eagerly licked his fingertips clean.

After they finished and she was cleaning herself off, Charlie stood back, laughing and shaking his head.

"What?" Julie asked.

"I knew you had slut in you, but...damn!"

Julie smiled. She liked it that he had called her a slut.

Charlie breathed a sigh of relief.

A few hours later, Julie found herself thinking about this new twist in her life and where it was leading. Even though the gangbang was great, she still couldn't help but feel that she was growing a little farther away from Charlie. Sure, he was a great lover and stud extraordinaire, but there just wasn't much else there besides the sex. She resolved to keep fucking him and going along with his scenarios, but should he ever try to insinuate himself into her life on any level deeper than that, then she would have to tell him. Charlie, on the other hand, would have been happy to hear this resolve of hers. It would have made him worry a lot less about keeping her attention. He had to meet his goal of turning her out otherwise Dave would think that he was simply up to no good all along. He didn't want that. If he didn't turn her into an absolute slut, he would probably have to leave town. He just wouldn't be able to face Dave or himself. Since he was running out of options, he decided that it was time to call in some help.

11

As Lucy watched Julie hunching and dancing with the oily-looking meathead out on the dance floor, she couldn't believe that she was actually involved in such a conspiracy. Here she was, taking prim and proper Julie into the Groove Orchard, which coincidentally also just happened to be the biggest meat market in town. It was the kind of club where you go expecting to hook up and if you don't, it's only because you're too drunk or get lost on the way to the meathead's car. Earlier that evening, while Julie had been at the food court eating lunch, Charlie had given her a directive. He had waited until he saw Julie leave because if he hadn't, she would have been all over him in the stock room and he wouldn't have had a chance to give Lucy her instructions. At least he hoped that was what would've happened.

"You know, I've been thinking," he started. "It's one thing for me to be whoring Julie out and fucking her three ways to Sunday, but what do you think would really make her into a bona fide slut?" Charlie knew that Lucy was pretty loose and would probably have a lot of insight into these matters.

Lucy thought for a minute.

"Well, me and my friends always go to the Groove Orchard and hook up whenever we're feeling horny. So, I guess a girl who really likes sex would go there and hook up."

Bingo! Charlie smiled.

"That's exactly the kind of thing I was thinking."

"So, I take it that you want me to take her to the club and let her get picked up?"

"Yep. You do that and I'll personally set up a gangbang just for you."

Lucy's body tingled at the thought of that. Since she had become involved in Charlie's project, she had gotten screwed so much by Charlie and his friends that she hadn't even thought about the Groove Orchard. That, and what she got from Julie at the store, was almost more than she needed. She had always had an enormous sex drive, so it was hard for her to believe that she was actually feeling sated. The great thing was that she really hadn't even had to do anything—aside from having sex with Julie—for Charlie except listen to his stories of what he had either done to her or what he was going to do to her. This usually led up to them fucking like dogs. It had been one heckuva sweet deal.

Julie writhed with the meathead on the floor for a little while before they both disappeared into the throngs of people. Lucy left to find them. It wouldn't be hard because, as she knew all too well, when two people hooked up at the Groove Orchard, they were going to either of two places: The car or the ladies room. Knowing how hot and heavy Julie was getting it on with the meathead on the dance floor, Lucy figured that the ladies room was the best bet. She knew that the poor girl wouldn't be able to wait out the walk to the car.

As Lucy made her way though the mass of writhing bodies, she was felt up repeatedly by the people on the dance floor. The people were packed so tight it was hard not to move without being pressed up against somebody. She was getting so turned on as she made her way to the ladies room that she knew that was going to have to hook up tonight or she would be so kinked up she wouldn't be able to see straight the next day. She couldn't help but stop to do a little writhing of her own with the various meatheads and girls she came into contact with. The smell of the sweat, perfume, cologne and pheromones was almost too much for her to take. Her breathing sped up and her body was sensitive to the touch by the time she made her way though the crowd.

Upon entering the restroom, she immediately began to look for Julie's feet underneath the stall doors. The smell of sex was strong in the room due to all the couples fucking, but nonetheless, she found them in seconds. One foot was up and from the moans coming from the stall, she knew that Julie was getting it in stork position. She quickly pulled out her cellphone and called Charlie.

"Well, she's doing it," Lucy whispered.

"Great," Charlie said, sounding slightly stoned.

"Well, what do you want me to do?"

"Well, you know what I'd do," Charlie chuckled. This was just so easy, he thought to himself. Why had he doubted his ability?

Lucy smiled. "Will do. Now that my mission is accomplished, you better have my gangbang set up for this weekend."

Charlie laughed. "Don't worry about it. It's my pleasure. Hell, I would have done it even if she had sat crying in the corner all night."

Lucy pushed the *end* button and put the phone back into her purse. She took a sip from a recently abandoned martini sitting on the sink and walked towards the stall. She could feel herself getting turned on just a little bit more with each step. This was going to be great. She thought about her upcoming gangbang just to put her libido into high gear. With no hesitation, she pushed the door open.

"Lucy!" Julie said, startled. The meathead looked up for a second and went back in without missing a breath. He didn't miss a stroke.

"Did you save some for me?" Lucy smiled.

Julie smiled back and put her hand on Lucy's shoulder to give her some support. Lucy moved in and began to kiss her on her neck, all the while getting wetter and wetter. Meanwhile, the meathead kept hammering Julie. Next, Lucy went to work on Julie's breasts, but she knew that she would have to have some of the meathead's dick before too long.

"Why don't you let me take a turn?" Lucy said, breathlessly.

"Just give me a second, okay? I'm about to come."

"Okay," Lucy said. She turned to the meathead. "You better save some for me, you hear?" She ordered him.

He looked at her with a blank stare of concentration and nodded.

Within a few seconds, Julie filled the restroom with screams of pleasure. When she was finished, she moved out of the way and let Lucy have him. Lucy had her panties off in seconds and moved into the spot where Julie had been just seconds before. Like a machine, the meathead went to work. Julie worked her breasts and rubbed Lucy's pussy while the meathead fucked her. Lucy was there in a few minutes, almost collapsing from her orgasm. After seeing that the girls had finished, the meathead continued on for a few seconds more before pulling out. Lucy and Julie eagerly got down on their knees and finished him off with their mouths, thirstily guzzling his semen.

After they got their clothes straight, Julie and Lucy walked back out to the dance floor. Both girls were still turned on and couldn't keep their hands off each other, but restrained themselves from going all out. The night was still young after all. The meathead walked out with them.

"Say, do you two girls want to go and get something to eat?" the meathead asked.

Lucy was kind of hungry so she was actually thinking of taking the guy up on his offer. After all, a free meal is a free meal. Besides, she wouldn't mind using the guy again later. He had been pretty good. However before she could accept, Julie made it clear that she other plans.

"No, we don't think so. We've got to hook up some more tonight. Right, Lucy?"

Lucy looked at her and smiled. Charlie was going to be so happy to hear this.

12

The next morning, Julie yawned and took a look around her. Where exactly was she? But then she remembered.

She was in some guy's room. Some guy she didn't know. The guy she had let pick her up the previous night at the club. After they had abandoned the meathead, she and Lucy had hooked up again almost immediately. This was after she had her fun in the restroom. Being tired of the noise and what not, she had readily accepted the guy's invitation to come over and examine his etchings. Of course, he had a friend, so it followed that Lucy was also invited. She had been at first a little apprehensive about going to some strange guy's apartment, but she was horny and he seemed nice enough. She hadn't even gotten his name, but he had a nice butt and looked like he might have a big cock, so that was good enough as far as she was concerned.

"I've got roommates, but they won't mind you coming," the guy said.

Julie didn't mind and neither did Lucy. Why should they? However, what the guy had neglected to tell them that he lived in a frat house.

Bleary eyed, she took a look around. No one was in the room except for she and Lucy. She looked down at herself. She was still completely naked. She looked over at Lucy who was still sound asleep and also naked. Then she remembered the bukkake and gangbang she and Lucy had received the previous night after they had arrived at the house. She shook her head and chuckled at just how wild things had gotten.

Lucy stirred a little when she heard Julie chuckling. She took a look around the room for a second and then remembered what had happened. Then she cracked up for no other reason than the fact that Julie was laughing.

After a little bit, when the girls were finally able to settle down, they began to put their clothes on.

"Wow, that was wild last night, wasn't it?" Lucy said as she searched around for her panties. "I mean I've been in some gangbangs before but nothing like that."

"There were just so many guys!"

"I guess we're both just a couple of sluts, don't you think?"

Julie laughed.

"No, we're not sluts. We're just a couple of girls who aren't afraid to have fun."

Lucy stopped and looked at her.

"We're sluts."

Both girls cracked up.

The previous night after they had arrived at the frat house, Julie was a little hesitant to continue. Sure, she had done almost everything there was to do sexually by this point but she still couldn't help but have a little trepidation about entering the frat house. Charlie had been present at her first gangbang, but in this case it was just she and Lucy. There's no way they could protect themselves if things got out of hand. Regardless, she decided to keep an open mind.

"You didn't tell me this was a frat house," Julie said.

"You didn't ask," Julie's guy said.

"I don't know about this," Julie said.

"Oh, c'mon. We're not going to do anything," Lucy's guy said.

"All that stuff that you've heard about frat houses isn't true," Julie's guy added, crossing his fingers behind his back.

Lucy was hoping that everything that she had heard about frat houses was true. She had heard that they were just a bunch of drunken, sex-crazed perverts who thought nothing of getting girls drunk and passing them around. She had been horrified when she had heard these stories before she had been turned out, but now when she thought about them she more than hoped that she would be able to have one of her own. Charlie would love this. He would owe her so much if she was able to get Julie ganged by all the frat guys.

"C'mon, Julie. These look like a bunch of nice guys to me," she lied. She could tell by the way her guy was leering at her that she was going to be in for some for something. What it was, she wasn't quite sure, but she hoped that it involved some of that stuff she had heard about.

Secretly, Julie was getting very excited about the prospect of going to into the house. She was already so horny that she couldn't stand still, but even so, she couldn't help but be a little intimidated by the all the frat guys. There were just so many of them. She wasn't sure she was ready for all of this.

"Okay, then," Julie said and the two girls followed the guys into the house.

Once inside the guys took them into a large room towards the middle of the house where a small party was going on. It looked like everyone was having fun except for the fact that no girls were there. It was just a bunch of guys sitting around and drinking beer.

Julie halted when she came to the door. Lucy noticed but continued to walk on in. A beer was put in her hand almost on cue as she entered the room.

Seeing that Lucy wasn't going to wait on her, Julie walked in too, reluctantly accepting a beer from one of the frat guys. She was feeling a little ill from all the drinking that she had been doing at the club earlier that night.

"Drink up," Lucy's guy said as he stood there beside Julie almost urging her to drink her beer so he could get her another.

"I'm not that thirsty," she said, a little queasily.

"I'm sorry. You're in Library Science, aren't you?"

"Yes," Julie answered, proudly.

"Yeah, everybody knows what wimps you guys are. I bet you can barely even finish that can."

Julie narrowed her eyes at the guy and her nausea immediately retreated. She wasn't about to let some frat boy make fun of her chosen profession.

"Oh, yeah?" She would show him. She turned the beer up and finished it without taking a breath. She glared at the guy in triumph.

"Give me another."

With that, the guy started handing her beers. As she drank, a crowd began to gather around her. After about her third beer, somebody started urging her to "Take it off!"

Since she was already sort of drunk, Julie couldn't see any real reason not to. She started peeling off her clothes.

Julie kept it up until she had drunk about a six pack, thoroughly impressing the guy and everybody else at the party. By this time she was also completely nude.

"Way to go, girl!"

After a couple of seconds, Julie realized that she had never been naked in front of a large crowd before. She was a little embarrassed, but not for longer than a couple of seconds. She began to enjoy the leering eyes on her. Lucy watched her from the other side of the room with a smile. Now it was just a matter of minutes before things would really get rolling.

Lucy took a big sip of her beer and walked over to where Julie was and started taking off her clothes too.

"Free blowjobs!" she yelled.

Julie looked at her amazement.

"Yeah, we're gonna give everyone here a free blowjob."

Julie smiled. That sounded nice.

"And if you're good enough, we'll even let you fuck us!"

Julie really started to squirm then. She couldn't believe she could be so lucky.

So, it began. Every guy in the place whipped out his dick. There were about fifteen of them and they each had a go. First they started out in a line, each one patiently waiting his turn, while Julie and Lucy finished them off. This lasted only as long as one person had one time through, after that, when the girls presented their pussies to the guys, it was katey-bar-the-door. They were like a bunch of dogs, doing whatever it took to get a spot. They pushed and shoved trying to get a hole. The ones that were forced to wait loudly urged the others on. They wanted them go ahead and finish so they get another turn.

By the time it was over, each guy had had at least three turns and Lucy and Julie were absolutely coated. What they didn't swallow was all over their faces and bodies. The girls had had so many orgasms they had lost track of them.

Julie had had a blast. She was beginning to feel that she was really suited for gangbanging.

As they finished dressing, Julie and Lucy looked around for their host.

"I don't see him anywhere."

"Let's leave," Lucy said. "You can thank him later."

"Okay," Julie said.

As they walked out of the house, stumbling over all the sleeping bodies littered throughout the place, they finally saw their guy passed out on the pool table.

"Do you think we should wake him up?" Julie asked.

"I don't think so. You can just come by here later," Lucy said hoping that Julie would make this a regular stop.

As they walked out onto the street Lucy couldn't wait to get home and call Charlie. However, Julie couldn't wait to get home and jump on Dave.

13

The next day, Julie arrived at the mall early. Lucy was feeling a little sick, or so she said. She had asked Julie to cover for her and of course, the good-natured girl had agreed to come on in. Normally, she had a class during this time, but thankfully, it had been cancelled. Otherwise, there would have been no one to open the store until four when one of the other part-time girls came in. She didn't really want to go to work, but figured that if Charlie was there to service her on her lunch break, it might make up for any inconvenience.

While Lucy had said she was sick, Julie somehow doubted it. The truth was that she was just too hung over to come in. Probably. Julie could never understand why it was always Lucy who called in sick the next day whenever they went out partying. It was getting kind of annoying.

Julie dodged the many strolling mall walkers as she made her way to the store. The mall was a haven for retired people to come and walk and congregate. While she had always had a respect for the elderly, sometimes these people were just too much for her to take. Usually, they would bully people out of their way while they were walking and heaven forbid that anyone accidentally sat in one of their chairs at the food court. A person would never hear the end of that. One of the things that really annoyed her was that they would always whistle at her whenever she walked past them. She rather enjoyed it whenever men whistled, but not when it came from a bunch of grandpas. It was just sort of creepy, she thought. Sometimes, Julie thought that all the old people were kind of like a pack of teenage boys. It was like they had their old people gang and they were going to do anything they could to keep a person off their turf.

Of course, Charlie was lurking around the store waiting for her when she arrived. He leaned, almost like he was posing, beside the store. He had one foot propped up and was smoking a cigarette—which was in strict violation of mall rules. It was the kind of thing that if Charlie saw someone else doing it, he would call the police. Of course, these rules didn't apply to him. It wasn't like this was actually his real job or anything. He didn't care if the place burned down as long as he was getting something out of it. However, he was a little surprised to see Julie. He was actually there to see Lucy and maybe act out some of the juicy details from the frat house incident. He had been so happy to hear about what had happened there that he had jerked off immediately and had kept a hard-on since. He was so pleased with himself he was almost floating. Sex wasn't the only reason why he wanted to see Lucy, though. He was also there to try to get some coffee money. He had spent all his money on beer the previous night and knew that Lucy would have some or would at least steal some from the register for him. At any rate, he wasn't disappointed to see Julie even though getting the money from her would be far trickier. She was just too honest. He immediately homed in on her tits and ass

"Hey, baby," Charlie said, moving in close and rubbing her pussy through her pants. "I hope you've got some of that left for me,"

Julie smiled and looked at Charlie's bulge. She was pleased by the sight of his hard-on. The fact that Charlie was always horny always amazed her. He could go all the time. He was different from Dave in that respect. Sometimes, it was obvious that Dave just wasn't in the mood.

"C'mon, Charlie. That's the kind of thing you always say. Surely, you've can come up with something besides that."

Charlie smiled. He would teach her about that smart mouth, just as soon as she got that store opened. And she gave him some money.

"You gonna open that store up or not? You know I don't like to wait."

Julie hurried to get the store open, because at the mere suggestion of what was to come, she started warming up. She could feel the juices flowing as she pushed up the gate.

After she got the gate up, Charlie started to walk into the store, but was rudely bumped by a mall walker.

"Get out of the way, asshole!" the old man said as he hustled his way past them.

Charlie thought for a second and started to get pissed off, but then he looked at Julie. Horny little Julie, all juiced up and ready for him. Then he got an idea about how to get his coffee money.

"Hey, Old Timer, come over here."

Julie saw what Charlie was about to do and started to cringe.

"No, Charlie! Don't do it!"

Charlie ignored her, and yelled again, "Hey, Old Timer!"

This time the old man stopped what he was doing and turned his hearing aid up.

"Hey, Old Timer!"

This time he heard. Quizzically like an old dog, he turned around and stared at Charlie. Charlie yelled at him again.

"C'mon back, old man! I've got something for you to watch."

Julie breathed a sigh of relief as she heard Charlie say the word "watch." This might be kind of fun.

The old man hustled over to the store and walked over to where Charlie and Julie stood.

"What did you want?"

"Do you want to see something good?"

The old man looked at him suspiciously.

"What is it? A game of some sort?"

Charlie smiled and Julie started breathing heavier at the prospect of finally getting some sort of release. She just hoped he would hurry.

"Give me five dollars and I'll let you watch us fuck."

The old man's eyes opened in amazement and he took a lecherous look at Julie. He immediately started to drool.

"It'll make that ancient prick of yours stand straight up," Charlie added.

"Okay," the old man wheezed.

"Give me the money first, Old Timer."

The old man hurriedly took out his money and handed it to Charlie.

"Now, just follow us back to the back here and find a place to get comfortable, because I'm gonna wear this girl out."

The old man followed them into the back room.

Julie was getting more and more aroused by the thought of an audience even though it was a dirty old man.

"Get your clothes off!" Charlie said as he started to pull down his pants.

Julie immediately obeyed and pulled off her skirt and top.

The old man's eyes got as big as saucers as he took a look at Julie's breasts. He started breathing hard as his hand immediately went to his pants and he started rubbing himself and grinning like a fool. This reminded him of when he used to sit in the closet and jerk off while he watched his wife screw the milkman, he thought to himself, Man! Them were the days! He was so excited by this memory he could barely see straight. He whipped it out and started stroking it, in earnest.

"C'mon, girl! Show me them big babies!"

Charlie couldn't help but chuckle.

It was amazing how excited the old man was becoming. Julie took a look at his erection and couldn't help but notice that he was hung like a horse. She knew she was going to have to take care of that thing too regardless of how old he was. A dick like that didn't come along every day.

However, just as she started going down on Charlie, the old man started gasping and clutching at his chest. Thinking that he was just excited, Julie and Charlie continued. After a couple more minutes, the old man's eyes rolled back into his head and he collapsed to the floor.

Julie and Charlie immediately stopped.

"Go get help!" Julie said as she went over to the old man who was lying comatose, dick still in hand. While she cared for him, she saw that his erection was still there. This gave her an idea. She immediately pulled it from his hand and started going down on him. Her efforts had an effect immediately. He started stirring as soon as she started sucking.

I'm doing it, she thought. I'm sucking him back to life.

She kept on even though it was hard to even get her mouth around it. It was that big.

As she sped up her assault on his penis, he started to groan. He began to moan as he moved closer to completion.

He stated moving a little more right before he suddenly stiffened up. Julie sensed his body tense and started sucking with all she had. It was just a matter of seconds before he exploded all over the back of her throat.

"Oh, my goodness!" He gasped as he regained consciousness.

He stared around like a wild man for a second before finally focusing on Julie. He took one look at her, there with his dick in her mouth and he fainted.

She managed to put his penis back in his pants just as the paramedics arrived. Charlie was hot on their heels, drinking a cup of coffee.

The old man came to right when they were strapping him in.

"That girl!" he said and pointed to Julie. "She saved me!"

Julie smiled to herself at her good deed and Charlie was pleased that he had remembered to get his five dollars up front.

14

As Julie got ready for church the following Sunday, she couldn't help but feel a little hypocritical. Here she was, going to Sunday school and just the previous week, she had been fucking like a street-whore.

She had never really considered sex with Dave to be a sin. She was in love with him and they didn't do it that often. When, they did, it was always very quick and very unspectacular. However, Charlie was a different story. With him, it was all about the fucking and whatever else he had made her do. She couldn't believe that one person could have had the power to turn her into such an animal. Sure, she was doing it mostly on her own now, but if it hadn't been for Charlie, she never would've known what she was missing. She still smiled whenever she thought about what had happened in the barbeque joint, the frathouse and everywhere else, for that matter. She started touching herself as she thought about all those guys all over her. She had never thought that it was possible for her to be so horny, but she had orgasmed more than she had believed possible with those guys. They had used her like she was the team slut and she had loved it. Gosh, she thought to herself, I really am turning into a whore. She was just going to have to reconcile her sexuality with her church activities the same way she had reconciled it with her relationship with Dave. She would just have to keep pushing ahead full tilt and let it work itself out.

She looked at herself in the mirror saw the beautiful girl looking back at her. She had only gotten as far as putting on her panties and bra. She couldn't help but put her hand in her panties and begin rubbing her clit. This had almost become an addiction for her. Since everything had started, she just couldn't stop masturbating. She masturbated at work. She masturbated in the car on the way home. She masturbated at lunch. She just couldn't stop. Today was no exception. She was so turned on she couldn't stand it. She wished that Dave or Charlie or somebody was here to give it to her the way she needed it. She was so horny that she just couldn't stand it. She just had to have something inside her. She looked around for something, anything to fill her void. Her fingers were not going to be enough this time. She didn't have a vibrator yet, but she made a mental note to buy one as soon as she could. She was going to have to do something. That was for sure.

She looked around. Her perfume bottles weren't big enough and her hair drier was too big. However, then her eyes rested upon her hairbrush. She smiled to herself. That would do.

She grabbed the hairbrush and lay down on her bed. Quickly she thrust the handle up her cunt and humped it until she quickly had an orgasm. When she was finished she licked the hairbrush handle clean. She loved the taste of herself. She couldn't wait until she could eat pussy again.

After relieving the pressure, Julie quickly got ready and went to church.

Dave had greeted her at the church door. He looked extremely handsome, she thought, in his brown wool-blend suit.

"I was beginning to think you weren't going to make it," Dave said, taking her hand.

"Well, I was a little distracted this morning," she said, smiling to herself.

"I'm glad you made it. This sermon is supposed to be a good one. Reverend Moody is gonna talk about Hell."

"Does he ever not talk about Hell?" Julie asked, a little annoyed.

Dave looked at her curiously, but didn't say anything else. They walked to their usual seat on their usual pew and settled into the service. That comment was certainly uncharacteristic, he thought. Charlie really was working on her.

As the service started, Julie looked around at all the pretty girls dressed up in their Sunday best and realized that this was going to be a very long service. She was getting turned on again, because she couldn't keep her mind from wandering from the girls' clothes to what was underneath them. She had to make a conscious effort not to start touching herself then and there in the church house. She knew she was going to have to keep her mind her mind focused. Surely, she could make it through a church service without masturbating.

It was an extremely good service, filled with all sorts of fire and brimstone and she tried her best to concentrate, but everywhere she looked, something reminded her of sex. The candles, the hard, wooden benches, even the organ reminded her of sex. She was conscious of the wet patch quickly developing on the bench beneath her.

She was relieved when the service finally let out. She quickly said her goodbyes and she hurried Dave up to his car.

"So, where do you want to eat?" Dave asked, opening her door.

"I don't care, let's just go," She said, quickly getting into the passenger seat.

"Okay," he said and got into the driver's side.

"So, how about ribs?" Dave asked as he pulled out of the church's parking lot.

Julie didn't answer, because she couldn't. Before he was able to repeat the question, she had his pants unzipped and his cock in her mouth. The question about the ribs had been entirely too much for her to handle

Dave moaned as she took him into her mouth.

"I don't know what's gotten into you, but I like it."

She continued to slurp, bringing his pre-cum up fast. She rubbed her clit as she sucked, bringing herself to the point of orgasm almost as quickly. She sucked a couple of minutes more until he came into her mouth. She came hard as well, but she was careful to swallow every drop of his cum, so as not to ruin the wool blend.

"Damn, girl. We're gonna have to start going to the Sunday night service too, if this is what church is gonna do to you."

She rolled her eyes.

"So, have you decided what you want to eat?"

She smiled to herself.

"Let's get something at the drive thru, I want you to take me to your place and fuck me."

Dave was almost overjoyed. Listening to Charlie had been the smartest thing he had done lately. Besides, proposing to Julie, of course.

15

Josie made her way to the back of the restaurant carrying the dishes over to the dishwashers' area. This really sucks, she thought. She waitressed part time at the steakhouse in order to fulfill her father's directive that she have a job. He still provided her with her cash, but he insisted that she work otherwise he wouldn't fork over the cash. It could've been worse, she realized. She might have had to actually live on what she earned as a waitress. However, with the money she got off Daddy and the odd porn mag shoots, she was able to do quite well. Of course, Daddy didn't know anything about the porn stuff.

"I want you to know what it's like to work and go to school. I want you earn your education. I want you to suffer just a little bit," he often said to her whenever she bitched about her job. "Life can not always be a good time and it's time you learned it."

It was kind of an odd situation, but so was her dad. He made a living being a motivational speaker and teaching the Dale Carnegie course. Therefore, it was natural that he would be obsessed with instilling values and teaching her lessons from his seminars. It was like she was some sort of walking experiment to see if the stuff he taught actually held any weight. So, she went along with his notions and ideas to humor him and to get her allowance. She desperately sought a job that would require her to work as little as possible. It had been tough. She had searched for weeks before she had finally hit paydirt. The steakhouse had been the best she could find. It actually required that she do something, but on the upside, she only had to work for a couple of hours a week. Getting the job had been tough, but due to a little quick thinking on her part, she was able to get the hours she wanted. She had to do a little finagling because there was no way that anyone would only hire her to work only two hours a week. She had offered to work only for tips, which was very attractive to the manager.

"Yeah, that sounds all well and good, but what good is that going to do me?" the manager leered. He was an overweight man in his early forties. He was greasy from hanging around the fryers too much and out of shape from sitting on his ass all day. Josie knew that he obviously didn't get much attention from the ladies, so she was dead-on when she played her trump card.

"Well...I could give you a blowjob," Josie said. Sure he was a little disgusting, but she couldn't afford to get cut off by her dad. She had no doubt that it would work because she knew that the way to a man's heart is not necessarily through his stomach.

Needless to say, that clinched the deal. In fact, he said that she didn't even have to work as long as she came in and occasionally gave him a blowjob. Of course, she said no to this. After all, she did want to earn her money. She wasn't a complete slacker. However, she complied with his wishes whenever he threatened to fire her. After she got used to him, she didn't mind the fact that he was greasy and overweight. It wasn't that big of a deal for her to service him, but she didn't let him know that. Still the time she spent at the restaurant was definitely the hardest two hours of her week.

As she walked over to the dishwasher, she couldn't help but overhear a conversation that the dishwashers were having.

"That girl!" one guy said. "Damn! She does it all, man!"

Josie's curiosity was instantly piqued. She thought for a second that they might be talking about her. She was a girl that would do it all. She didn't know how these dishwashers would know anything about her, but people do talk.

"Shiiit! You should have seen her at the barbeque place. She did everybody! She even did it while she was eating ribs! Shit!"

Josie thought back. She hadn't eaten any barbeque in quite a while. She had recently tried going vegetarian, so any sort of barbeque place was out of the question. Maybe she had sleepwalked...

"Damn that Julie's fine! I heard that she gets mad if you don't fuck her!"

Julie? Julie? Josie thought to herself. Could they be talking about her Julie? Surely not. Sure, she and Julie had become quite intimate over the last little while, but Julie was still a good girl. She wouldn't do anything like that. It just wasn't in her. She went to church and everything. She just didn't believe it.

"I heard she works at the mall," one of the guys said.

"No, man, my cousin said she works at the library. He ought to know. He's going to college on a basketball scholarship. He said she sucked him off in one of the study rooms."

Mall! Library! Study rooms! It was Julie! Her Julie! At first she was shocked. How could her Julie do such a thing! She had certainly misread the girl. That was for certain. There was no denying that.

Josie went back out to the dining room and to the wait station. It was a little kiosk in the back of the restaurant where the wait staff refilled drinks and rolled silverware when things were slow. Josie never learned how to roll silverware. She wasn't there long enough to pick it up. Instead of working, she poured herself some tea and lit a cigarette. The other waitresses gave her a mean look. They were a little pissed off that she was able to get away with so much. The only thing that kept them from beating her up in the parking lot was the fact that they knew that she would only be there for a couple of hours.

"Lazy, rich bitch," an overweight waitress in her forties said to Josie as she wedged her way into the kiosk to refill her pitcher. "They ought to fire you and split up your paycheck between us."

Josie didn't even notice her. She was too lost in her own thoughts. Besides, she didn't even get a paycheck.

The fat woman huffed off when she saw that Josie wasn't paying any attention to her. Josie poured herself some more tea. As she smoked her cigarette, she thought about Julie. Here she was, thinking that Julie was all Miss Pious and Prim and Proper and everybody else knew that she was an absolute slut. Josie was a little hurt that Julie hadn't shared this part of her life with her, but there was something else about the revelation that bothered her. It was a feeling that completely surprised her. It was envy. She envied the fact that Julie was out there getting it from whoever she felt like. Julie was supposed to be a good girl, too! She wasn't even supposed to know about this stuff, much less be out there doing it.

If all this is true, what does it say about me, she thought. Here she was, this supposedly wild girl and she wasn't doing anything remotely like that. Sure, she was going out to the clubs, posing for magazines and getting laid occasionally, but Julie was out there getting gangbanged on a regular basis! Josie had only been gangbanged once and that had been by the football team when she was in high school. Those guys were so young and stupid that they didn't know what the hell they were doing. They barely knew which hole to stick it in. How she had even managed an orgasm was still a mystery to her. The possibility of such a thing hadn't presented itself to her since. That made her start wondering. How did opportunities like that even present themselves to Julie? Maybe it was the library thing? She didn't know, but did know one thing. She was definitely going to confront Julie about this stuff and let her know how she felt.

And she was going to ask her to take her along the next time she went out.

16

"I've got an opinion about that Charlie," the Librarian said as she ashed her cigarette.

She and Julie were sitting in her office talking. Julie was at the library for her lab, but since becoming acquainted with the Librarian on a more intimate basis, she hadn't really done anything as far as schoolwork went. For her lab time, she just went into the Librarian's office and they either had sex or talked about it. It was a pretty easy grade. During the course of one of their conversations, she had confided to the Librarian about Charlie and what he had been doing to her. She had also told her about Dave and how much better her sex life was since all this had started.

"What's wrong with him?" Julie asked, a little panicked. "I just knew that there was something wrong with this situation."

The Librarian smiled and exhaled.

"There's nothing wrong. I just don't think that you fully understand what's going on here."

Julie listened with rapt attention. The whole situation was a bit puzzling for her. After all, one minute she had been wholesome, apple pie Julie and the next she was the wild insatiable sexual creature.

"He's turning you out," the Librarian said, matter of factly.

Julie thought for a second. "What's that mean?"

The Librarian thought for a minute, trying to think of a good way to explain the situation.

"He's breaking you in. You know like you have to do with a pair of shoes? They're not always comfortable when you put them on, but the more you wear them, the better they get."

A light went off in Julie's head.

"So, he's making me do this stuff...so I'll like it?"

The Librarian nodded.

"Well, he's doing a great job because I absolutely love it."

The Librarian ashed again. "He's making you crave it."

"You're right! I do crave it!" Julie exclaimed. "I mean sex with Dave is great, but I've got to have more than that. I just don't know what I would do now if it wasn't for Charlie. I never know what kind of crazy thing he's going to set up."

The Librarian grinned because she was the same way. She loved a wide variety of sexual practices. Normal sex just didn't cut it anymore.

"But why would he pick me?"

The Librarian got up and walked over to her. She cut a striking figure in her tight black business suit. It was definitely a fetish get-up, although most people were too square to understand it. She stood behind the girl and played with her hair as they talked.

"I don't know. There's any number of reasons. Maybe he just saw you and thought that it would be good for you. A lot of guys are like that. They'll see some prim and proper young lady and want to turn her into an absolute slut. I know that's what happened to me."

"Maybe that's it," Julie sighed. "I'm just glad it happened, that's all I have to say. I mean he has the most wonderful cock. It's huge! Whenever I just think about it, I start getting wet."

The Librarian nodded. "I've known guys like that. They're so gorgeous that you don't know whether you want to suck, fuck or just look at them. From the sound of him, this Charlie sounds like somebody I would definitely like to meet in person. That cock of his sounds amazing."

"I'll bring him to your party. That is, if you invite me again."

"Nonsense. You're always invited to my parties. "

"Thanks," Julie said and continued, "Also, I didn't even know I liked girls before him. I'm kind of mad at myself because of all that I was missing out on."

"People really limit themselves by not considering all their options. I mean, I was just like you. I didn't know I liked women either, but now I couldn't imagine it any other way."

"I'm getting that way."

"Does you boyfriend know about all this?" the Librarian asked as she continued to play with her hair.

"Oh, no!" Julie said standing up. "He doesn't have any clue!"

The Librarian raised her eyebrow. That didn't sound quite right. There was no way that a girl who was doing all the crazy kind of stuff that Julie was wouldn't become a sexual monster in the bedroom. He would have to notice. If not, he was either dead or gay.

"But he has noticed the change in your sex life, though right?"

"I'm sure he has," Julie said as she sat down. "I mean we do it every which way now. Before, we rarely did it at all." She giggled. "I was so silly. I wouldn't let him even touch me unless it was some sort of special occasion or something. "

"Does your boyfriend know this Charlie character?"

"I don't think so."

"Hmmmm…" The Librarian thought for a second.

"Why what are you thinking?"

"Oh, nothing."

The Librarian thought some more. Something just wasn't adding up about the whole situation and she was pretty sure that she knew what it was. From her past experience in swinging and screwing all kinds of people, her intuition told her that Dave was probably involved in some way. That was just the way this was usually done. She had seen this kind of thing many times before.

Julie thought for a second. "So, do you think I should tell Dave?"

"I wouldn't," the Librarian said. If she was right about Dave, she was pretty sure that he must have some sort of end game cooked up. Most likely it wouldn't be anything bad, so she thought it best just to leave things alone. If it was, she would take care of Dave personally.

"Really? Why not? I would have thought you would've said that I should."

"Oh, I don't know. I'll tell you this, though. When you do decide that you're comfortable with him knowing, you need to break him in gently with this, so he's not too overwhelmed."

Julie thought for a second.

"So, you're saying that I should turn him out?" she giggled.

The Librarian smiled. "Yes, in a manner of speaking. Yes."

"That's funny. I don't think I'll ever tell him though. I'm just not sure he could handle it. I mean, he just knows me as a church girl. He would probably have a heart attack if he found out."

"Maybe," the Librarian said, although in her gut, she knew that he wouldn't.

17

Dave picked Julie up that night at the library. They had a dinner date with his parents. They were going to discuss the upcoming wedding a little more in detail While Julie liked Dave's parents, she couldn't help but be a little put off by them They were very unlike Dave in the fact that they were sort of crude. Compared with the rest of the world, he was sort of an ordinary joe, but compared to them, he was actually quite refined. Then again, he had spent a lot of time with his grandparents and had gone into the Marines right out of high school.

Dave walked in, took a look around for Julie and saw her in the Librarian's office. Julie saw him through the window and waved for him to come in. After introductions were made, the couple left. After meeting him, the Librarian was still convinced that Dave was involved in turning Julie out. It was a textbook case, as far as she was concerned. She thought about what Julie had been doing and the idea of a sweet young girl like Julie being used like that became too much for her to take so she went over behind her desk and masturbated. Her hand was out of sight from everyone in the library.

Dave was extremely excited that night for some reason, Julie noticed. He was all fidgety and talking a mile a minute. What she didn't know was that Charlie had updated him about her gangbang at the frat house and he was so stoked he could barely keep it in his pants. He was all hands as they walked to his car.

"You're certainly frisky tonight," Julie said, welcoming his hands on her.

"It must be the weather or something," he said.

When they got to the car, which was parked on the other side of the campus, Julie immediately unzipped his pants and began sucking him off. He came within seconds. She swallowed every drop but not before making sure to lick him clean. This was beginning to become a routine. It seemed as though every time they met now, she immediately gave him a blowjob. Dave certainly didn't mind. As far as Julie was concerned, she thought it was a nice thing to do. She loved the taste. She just wished there was more.

His mind now clear, Dave drove them out to his parents' house. It was out in the suburbs, in the older working class part of town. The houses were a little rundown, but still kept up for the most part. However, from all the K-cars and older model Camaros, it was obvious that this place was home to some rough trade. His parents were no exception.

"Hi, hon," Dave's mom, Greta, greeted them at the door. She was in her late forties, skinny as a bone and wore exceptionally tight, revealing clothes. Her hair had been fried by too many perms and she was constantly smoking Virginia Slims. Dave had told her that his mom thought that women's cigarettes were elegant.

"Hi, Greta," Julie said, cringing at the hug the woman gave her. The smell of cheap perfume and stale cigarette smoke was almost too much for her allergies to bear.

As they walked into the living room, the noise from the television was almost too much to bear. Ernie, Dave's dad, was watching a porno movie and apparently hadn't noticed them come in. This kind of behavior wasn't very unusual for him. He rarely acknowledged anyone except when it was convenient for him to do so. These rare occasions were when someone owed him money. He would also become quite conversational whenever he was trying to talk himself out of a jam.

"Ernie! Turn that damned thing off! I can't even hear myself think!" Greta yelled at him as she threw a pillow and hit him the head.

Ernie grunted and turned the TV down. He turned around and stared at them.

"Hey, Dad. How's it going?"

Ernie grunted and turned back to the TV.

"He's not feeling good. He's got the shits."

Julie smiled politely. These people were so different from her parents. Her father was a church deacon and her mother was the church organist. They were so reserved that they could barely even speak to themselves.

"C'mon into the kitchen. I've already got the chicken ready," Greta said.

Julie looked and sure enough there were a couple of buckets of Kentucky Fried Chicken sitting on the table. Whenever Dave's parents invited them for dinner, it was always Kentucky Fried Chicken. Dave had explained that the reason for this was because his mother was such a terrible cook. She wanted to spare Julie the horror of eating her cooking. He, of course, neglected to mention that she also hated to cook.

After they were seated and Ernie's porno was finished, they sat down to eat. Of course, it was every man for himself and the food was quickly dispersed to all the plates. Julie got stuck with a leg. Quickly the subject of their wedding came up.

"We're not going to have to pay for anything are we?" Greta asked.

"Oh, no, Mom, I'm taking care of everything," Dave said to quickly assuage his mother's concerns. She was always very concerned that her children would make her pay for something. It seemed to be a fear for her as she would always refuse to pay for anything when in their presence. Dave and his sister, as a result, rarely participated in any sort of family get-togethers.

"Good, good," Greta said, unselfconsciously. "I really hope it's a big wedding then. I just want the best for you."

"Thanks, Mom," Dave said obliviously.

They ate for a little while longer without any saying anything.

"Honey, I don't mean to ask you a personal question, but you're not a virgin are you?" Greta asked.

Julie almost spit up her mashed potatoes and gravy. Her face grew red.

"Mom! That's no kind of question to ask," Dave protested.

Ernie gave her a contemptuous look that indicated that he had heard some of the rumors going on about her, but he didn't say anything.

"Oh, I'm sorry, dear. I didn't mean anything. I was just hoping that she wasn't. You know what they say about shopping around and all."

"Mom!"

Julie turned a little redder. If they only knew, she thought to herself.

"I just don't want her to get tired of you and run off with the first thing that pays any attention to her."

"Mom!" Dave yelled again, embarrassed for his family, but relived for the fact he had listened to Charlie about this subject.

"Okay, then. Who's going to be your best man? Is it going to be that guy you were in the Marines with? What's his name...?"

It was Dave's turn to spit out his potatoes as she almost said Charlie's name.

Julie noticed Dave's odd behavior.

"What's wrong? Are you choking?"

"No... I just swallowed the wrong way, "Dave gasped.

Dave didn't have to worry because Ernie abruptly got up and left the table. He had feasted like a locust and was now going back to the television. Of course, this didn't set well with Greta who was trying to have a normal family time in her own weird way. She ran after him, screaming about what a worthless human being he was.

After she was gone, Julie turned to Dave.

"Your parents are crazy."

"I know."

He thought for a second, deciding to change the subject.

"Do you think I could get another blowjob?"
She smiled and got ready for dessert.

18

After leaving his parents' house, Dave and Julie were barely able to make it back to his apartment. They already had their clothes half off before they were up the steps and were going at it like dogs before he had the key in the door. For some reason, the two of them were so horny they couldn't get off fast enough. Julie devoured his cock and cum with her pussy and mouth, never getting her fill. She was such a wild woman, that Dave was amazed that he was even able to keep up with her.

After laying there for an hour, Julie looked at her watch.

"Well, I've got to get back. I've got a paper to work on."

"Work on it here," Dave said.

Julie smiled. "You know I can't do that. If I stay here, I won't get anything done." She reached over and grabbed his dick.

He laughed.

After getting dressed, Dave walked her to the door. After she left, he shut the door behind her, and smiled to himself.

Outside the apartment, Charlie was waiting. He was beside himself with anticipation. He had another scheme cooked up that he couldn't wait to try out on her. This would really set her off even more, he though.

He watched Julie walk out of the apartment building from behind some bushes. Her clothes were all rumpled and hair was all disheveled. He chuckled. He could see that she had been fucking again. He liked knowing that she was getting so she couldn't get enough.

As she crossed the street to her car, Charlie stepped out from behind the bushes.

She jumped a little bit, but when she saw it was him, her face flushed. He couldn't believe it. She was blushing to see him.

"Oh, it's you," she said and walked shyly over to him.

"I see you've been fucking," he said, coolly.

"Is it that obvious?"

He nodded and smiled. He walked over to her and put his arm around her and pulled her in tight to him. She didn't resist. She put her arms around him, but not before quickly looking back at the apartment to see if Dave was watching. He put his hand on her ass and rubbed it. God, she had a tight little ass.

"You want to go back to my place and meet someone?" he murmured into her ear.

She thought about her paper and considered declining, but then realized what going back to his place meant. She decided to go. She could always do the paper tomorrow. It wasn't due for another two weeks. Surely, she could let it wait. Besides, who was she going to meet? It would probably be somebody hung like a horse and ready to really put it to her. Maybe it would be another black guy. She had especially liked that.

"I'll go, but only if you promise that you're gonna fuck me absolutely stupid."

Charlie laughed.

"You don't have to worry about that."

"Well, let's go."

They got into Charlie's truck and drove about ten miles into one of the cities older residential areas to Charlie's place. This was the first time she had ever been to it and she wasn't very impressed. He lived in an old, two-story, wooden house that had seen better days. It still looked somewhat liveable though and it was easy to tell how beautiful it once was.

"If you fixed this place, it would be absolutely gorgeous."

Charlie looked at her incredulously.

"I think it looks fine."

She groaned to herself and realized why she would never have anything more than a sexual relationship with Charlie.

After she got out of the truck, she started towards the front door.

"Julie, we're not going in that way."

"Why's that?"

"That way's boobytrapped. Only people who I don't know try to go in the front door."

She rolled her eyes and followed him around to the back door. If it wasn't for that cock...

Inside the house was an absolute mess. Old newspapers and junk were everywhere. She also noticed lots of empty pizza boxes and TV dinner refuse. There was also an abundance of porn lying about. She noticed that on one of the magazines, there was a girl who looked sort of like Josie. She quickly dismissed that thought, though. It had to be a coincidence.

"Most of this stuff was here when I moved in," Charlie explained nervously, trying to come up with some reason why his place was such a sty.

"Ever thought about throwing it out?"

"I will when I have a chance to go through it. I've only lived here for a year." That part at least was true.

Julie didn't care, though. It wasn't like she was going to marry him or anything. She was here for one reason and she wanted to get the show on the road. She walked over to Charlie and grabbed him by the crotch.

"So, when are you gonna start fucking me?"

He removed her hand.

"I'll fuck you after I've introduced you to a friend of mine," Charlie said, trying to sound official, like he meant business. He was so excited though that he almost started giggling. He could barely wait.

Julie's eyes lit up.

"Is he gonna fuck me too?"

"It's not a he, it's a she. And she will do whatever she wants with you."

Hmmmm... Julie thought, that sounds fun.

"Now, take your clothes off and follow me upstairs. We're going to do things a little differently this time."

She willingly obeyed, giddily anticipating what new way he was going to find to use her body.

They ascended the stairs and went into a big room which was empty of furniture except for a couple of wooden chairs.

"Go over to the wall."

She looked at him curiously, wondering exactly what his game was, but when she looked at the wall, she knew what was going on. A set of chains were attached to the plaster. She took them in her hands and turned to him.

"What are these for?"

"I think you know," he said, quickly tried to regain his composure.

This was just so kinky, she couldn't resist. She eagerly put the chains on her hands and feet. She wasn't going anywhere now.

"Are you gonna blindfold me, too?" she asked anxiously.

He shook his head.

"No blindfold," he said. "Now, you can meet your new best friend. Come on out, Ingrid."

With that, a tall blonde woman dressed in a leather dominatrix outfit walked into the room. She had short hair and was built like a brick shithouse. She was also carrying a riding crop. Julie instantly got wet at the sight of her. She was absolutely gorgeous. She was also Charlie's first ex-wife, but he didn't let her know it. He had brought her over from Germany with him. After she had gotten her citizenship, she had promptly divorced him. He was okay with it, though since she still let him fuck her occasionally. She had recently gotten into the dominatrix game and was doing pretty well. She had promised to come over and help him if he gave her his air conditioner. Since his air conditioner wasn't working, it was sweet deal for him.

"I've got a new one here for you, Ingrid. This one is a regular little slut."

"Ooohh…she looks like such a good girl, though. Are you sure about her?" Ingrid asked in a slight German accent.

Charlie laughed and detailed all of Julie's exploits. Julie felt her face turning red as he told Ingrid all the juicy details.

Ingrid smiled and you could see that she was going to enjoy this. She might have to see if Charlie had anything else she needed.

Without a word, Ingrid walked over to Julie and slapped her on the ass hard with her riding crop.

"Ow! That hurt!"

"Good. Little tramps like you need to be punished."

Ingrid slapped her ass again and again. Julie's ass was quickly turning red, but the more her butt hurt, the wetter she got. Her ass was hurting but she wanted to be fucked. She felt herself losing control as her ass was beaten. She came after about the tenth stroke. Her orgasm throbbed with each successive swat.

But Ingrid was now ready for some more.

"Stick your ass out."

Julie readily obeyed.

Ingrid rubbed her red ass with her gloved hand, and slowly worked her thumb into Julie's asshole. She roughly put her fingers in Julie's pussy and worked both holes to Julie's delight. Julie writhed against her fingers, juicing onto the hardwood floor. Ingrid next got down on her hands and knees and began licking Julie's cunt. Her face was quickly coated with Julie's fluid.

"Damn! I thought you were gonna fuck her, Ingrid."

Charlie tossed Ingrid a strap-on dildo which she quickly put on after she removed her clothes. Julie yelped as Ingrid rammed it into her ass and came for the second time. Ingrid fucked her ass like a wild woman.

"Fuck me, you little slut! Fuck me!" Ingrid grunted, her German accent becoming more pronounced.

This became too much for Charlie as he watched and stroked his cock. He walked over behind Ingrid and shoved his member into her pussy as she pumped Julie's ass. She came instantly and Julie came again. They were like some kind of strange animal, all writhing together.

"Put that thing in my pussy," Julie gasped as Ingrid paused while she came.

Ingrid slapped her ass and pulled the dildo out and moved it to her pussy and pumped it even harder than she had the ass.

Julie's eyes rolled back in her head with the ecstasy of what was going on. She felt like she was going to explode from the sexual tension.

After taking care of Ingrid for a while, Charlie realized that he wanted to give it to Julie a little bit before she became too spent.

"I thought you were never gonna stick that thing in me," Julie said as he shoved his dick into her twat.

Ingrid sat down beside them and turned the dildo on herself and worked it in and out like a woman possessed.

Charlie pistoned Julie's cunt to a froth and when the girl clamped her nails into his thighs, he realized that he couldn't handle it anymore. He pulled out and came all over the girl's ass. Ingrid readily lapped up the cum.

Charlie collapsed onto the floor, while Julie hung exhausted from the chains on the wall. He looked up at the girl and realized that while his job was almost done. Julie, though, was probably just getting started.

19

It didn't take a lot of finagling for Josie to get Julie to invite her along on one of her jaunts. In fact, it was Charlie who had suggested it.

After she had heard all the stories she had been absolutely dying to experience what Julie was experiencing. At least what she had heard that Julie was experiencing. At her first opportunity, she had asked. When Julie acted like she didn't know what Josie was talking about, Josie had begged. Julie was at first a little put off that her behavior was so publicly known, but she couldn't help but be a little flattered. Just so long as Dave didn't find out.

It all started because Charlie had begun to hear stories about Julie circulating around town. People were talking about her in locker rooms and construction sites throughout the city. She was beginning to get quite popular and he realized that he would definitely be losing his grip on her pretty soon so he had better make the most of it while he could. In fact, he even considered making her start an amateur porn website, but didn't really know html and had no motivation to learn. He had some mixed feelings about the realization that he was losing control of her. He had really gotten off on being able to make her do whatever he wanted by virtue of her eagerness to have sex with him. The same went with Lucy, but she already had been turned out long ago. He enjoyed having this power over women, however, he especially enjoyed having it over Julie. She was such a good girl before he got a hold of her. He just loved making her be bad. He sighed at the fact that soon she would be going out on her own and he and his cock would just become a distant memory.

He had been at his house thinking about all the good times that he was having with Julie and wondering why in the hell wasn't he screwing her that night. When he had told her to meet him at the park that night, she had said that she was meeting Dave for an engagement party. He knew this wasn't true, because he had called Dave to check the story. Dave was putting up a satellite dish at his parents' house and Julie had told him that she couldn't go with him because she had to work late. Dave had naturally thought that Charlie was turning her out and Charlie had thought that she was being all lovey dovey with Dave. This is when Charlie had a flash. That little whore, he thought. She was lying to both of them because she was probably going out slutting on her own!

He didn't tell Dave what was going on, because he didn't want to sound like he wasn't doing what he promised. He assured Dave that he had some real major shit lined up for her, so he should be expecting her to come home and jump his bones. Dave said he couldn't wait. After he had hung up the phone with Dave, he realized that he had to come up with a plan for her tonight. He looked at his clock and saw that he didn't have much time. He would have to come up with it in the car. On the way over to Julie's dorm, he passed by the Triangle, an upscale lesbian bar and had an idea.

The Triangle was the bar of choice for the city's lipstick lesbian professionals. It was a place for the beautiful people and if you didn't look a certain way, you would get the cold shoulder to such a degree that would make you never come back again. Of course, Charlie didn't know any of this. He just knew that it was a lesbian joint.

Julie and Josie were getting ready to go out to the club when he arrived at their dorm room door.

"Charlie, what are you doing here? I told you that I...had..." Julie started, finding it hard to look him in the eye.

Charlie just shook his head. He decided against letting her know that he knew what she was up to.

"Don't worry about that thing. I think I know something you'll enjoy a lot more."

Josie looked at Julie.

"Maybe we should listen to him. This is that guy you were telling me about, isn't it?" She immediately looked down at the front of his pants, trying to gauge if Julie was telling the truth about the size of his cock.

Julie had told Josie all about how Charlie had opened up her eyes and legs to the world of recreational sex. Josie had sat wide-eyed, listening to every word and feeling a bit jealous that it wasn't her that all that stuff was happening to. But like she had realized at the restaurant, the only way for her to get over her slight feelings of resentment was to go out there and do it too. She was so looking forward to going out with Julie and now that Charlie was here, it appeared that her desires were going to be fulfilled. She also secretly hoped that after she had Julie had bonded as sluts, she might be able to persuade her to go on a photo shoot with her.

"Okay, Charlie. What is it?" Julie said. "It had better be good, because Josie really wants some action."

Charlie smiled and revealed his plan. He wanted the both of them to initiate an all girl gangbang at the Triangle.

Josie almost started salivating at the prospect of it. In fact, her eyes almost glazed over. Julie could feel herself heating up almost immediately.

"But how would we do something like that?" Julie asked.

"The same way as you did at all those other places. Most people are dying to do something like that. All it takes is one person to start it."

"I've heard that it's a little stuffy there, but there's a lot of beautiful girls. My cousin is a lesbian and she goes there all the time," Josie said.

"Just go in and give them a show. They'll come around. Two good looking girls like you two will have the place torn up in no time.

Even though she hadn't been that experienced for very long, Julie knew that he was right. She looked over at Josie and realized what a thrill it would be for her to be out there in the center of everything, turning on the crowd to such an extent that all their inhibitions would be lost. All sense of public decorum would be lost in a sex-filled frenzy.

"C'mon ladies, live a little," Charlie coaxed.

"We'll do it," they said together.

Charlie rubbed his hands with anticipation at the very idea of it, happy that he was able to pull it off.

20

Charlie dropped Julie and Josie off at the front door of the Triangle with the explicit order not to come out until the crowd was in a sexual frenzy. He wanted pussies dripping and mouths eating. He wanted full details. He would have gone in, but didn't want his appearance to put a damper on things. He figured that his presence would probably be an inhibiting factor and make some of the lesbians a little more self-conscious than usual.

Julie and Josie walked into the bar and immediately everybody's jaw dropped and their tongues subsequently hit the floor. The girls were dressed in identical little black dresses that clung to their bodies like cellophane. Everything could be seen, every curve and crevice. Their five inch heels accentuated their legs and they couldn't help but to turn every head in the place.

Their drinks were paid for before they could even make their way to the bar. It seemed as though every woman there had already bought them one.

The bartender asked them to take their pick. With all the drink offers, they pretty much had an open bar.

Julie smiled and ordered a martini while Josie ordered a red wine.

"Thanks," Julie said as she took a sip and lit a cigarette. She had recently taken up smoking, thanks to Charlie. He said he liked it when she had something in her mouth. She surveyed the crowd and realized that Josie was right. The place was filled with beautiful women. From the rustling and energy in the room, it was obvious that they were all horny as hell. Most of them were in conservative attire, but if one looked beyond the glasses and buns, it was obvious to see that this was an above average group of women as far as looks went. It was the kind of women that most bi-curious girls hope to have an experience with. She looked over at Josie and from her half-open lips and the way that she crossed and uncrossed her legs, she knew that she was thinking the same thing.

Julie was already wet so she knew that she was leaving a patch on the seat. She adjusted herself so that anybody watching her would be able to see up her dress. It was obvious that all eyes were on them so she decided to go ahead and get the show started.

"You ready?" she asked Josie.

Josie nodded.

With that, the two girls got up and walked to the vacant dance floor. Since it was still somewhat early in the evening, no one was drunk enough to start dancing. A slow song with a beat played as Josie and Julie began to dance suggestively. They danced close and caressed each other's bodies. They really turned up the heat for the girls and it was obvious that every single one of them was feeling it. This was definitely an enjoyable experience and when the crowd finally got going, it would be even better, Josie thought.

Charlie obviously knew his stuff because after a few minutes, they were joined by another couple. It was a statuesque blonde and a beautiful Latina. They danced even more suggestively than Josie and Julie. They were so close that they were almost intertwined and moved in close to Julie and Josie. It was as though the two couples were dancing with each other, they were so close. Pretty soon more couples joined and the dance floor filled up not long after.

As the couples danced, Josie and Julie became so turned on that they began to writhe against each other and anyone else they came into contact with. They pulled their dresses up as they hunched against each other, grinding to the beat of the music. Immediately some of the women took the cue and started to do likewise. It was true. No matter what kind of people there are in a crowd, a majority wants to get crazy and get it on. All it takes is one person to start it.

Feeling that the seed was planted, Julie began to undress Josie and kiss her neck. She then took off her own dress and soon both girls were naked. They began to go at it on the dance floor as if no one was there. Their lips and hands were all over each other's breasts, pussies and asses. They only recognized that other people were around whenever Julie finally invited the other women to join them. By that time, almost half the women on the dance floor were naked and the other half were in the process of getting naked. Julie looked out into the bar and saw that people were going at it left and right.

She couldn't help but smile. It was on!

It didn't take long for a full-fledged orgy to begin. Pretty soon Julie couldn't tell whose hands were on her. It was just like the times with the guys but this time the skin was so much softer and the hands were gentler. The floor was alive with writhing bodies as the women swapped partners with each other. Julie didn't even know who she was eating whenever a pussy presented itself to her. She just knew that what she wanted was coming from every direction and there was more than enough to go around. She had orgasm after orgasm as head after head took turns working on her down there. Josie had given her the first one but she had soon moved on to other beautiful girls. There were so many tits and asses that she couldn't keep up with everything she wanted to do. She thought that she was going to faint at one point from the sexual overload. She was so horny that she couldn't even get it fast enough and her face was glazed from the amount of pussy she had eaten. She positioned herself so her legs were scissoring those of the beautiful Latina and started hunching her as hard as she could. The Latina responded in kind and bucked her like a bronco. It didn't take long for them both to have massive shrieking orgasms.

Meanwhile, Charlie waited outside for them. He nervously smoked cigarettes and stroked himself with anticipation at what was going on inside the bar. After a few hours of waiting, he realized that the plan was such a success that they weren't coming out. That made him so uncontrollably horny that he immediately went home and called Lucy. He had hoped to get his hands on both Julie and Josie while they were worked up, but he realized that would have to wait for another day.

21

A few weeks later, as she crossed and uncrossed her legs repeatedly while they sat at the restaurant waiting to be seated, Dave couldn't help but notice the change that had taken place in Julie. Before, she had always been kind of timid and shy and hesitant to stand out in a crowd, but now, no one could possibly infer that she was shy, especially by looking at the outfit she was wearing. She wore an extremely short tight black skirt which barely covered her ass. It left nothing to the imagination and she made no attempt to hide the fact that she wasn't wearing any panties. It almost seemed as though she wanted everyone to know it, from the way she was sitting. She wore a tight, white, low-cut top through which her lovely brown nipples showed. All this, along with her four-inch classic pumps made her the center of attention in the lobby of the restaurant. Every man's and most womens' eyes were on her and it was obvious that it wasn't the food that was making their mouths water.

But it wasn't just that, her attitude had changed. Of course, she now was sexually insatiable and demanded to be fucked constantly. She was always unzipping his pants and sucking his cock. Sometimes he had to make up an excuse to leave because he just didn't have enough juice to continue. No, it was more than that. It was her attitude about life. She was so much more fun-loving and less serious now. It was as though her priorities had changed. Before she had always been so concerned about her studies and her job at the mall that she had never allowed herself to have any fun. He had always been canceling weekend trips and mini breaks that he had planned because either she had volunteered to work additional shifts or had to study. None of that was happening now. She was more concerned with herself now, not just what she thought the world expected of her. She had never allowed herself to be the sexual being that she was inside. She had been stifled. That was a different story now. He smiled to himself at the change and wondered if she knew that he had noticed the changes. He was sure that she hadn't, otherwise she would have made somewhat of an effort to conceal her behavior. He couldn't help but notice that whenever they were out, she checked out every person that passed before her eyes. He could tell that whenever she saw a hot chick or guy that she would start crossing the legs and her mouth would open just a little. He knew why she would disappear to the restroom or find some excuse to get away for a few minutes while she cornered the object of her affection. He could also tell when she wasn't successful because she would be all over him in the car on the way home.

Of course he had had his trepidations about handing her over to Charlie, but his gut told him that it was the right thing to do. He had worried about what would happen and how she would feel about him. He had actually considered calling Charlie back afterwards and telling him to call it off. However, he decided to sleep on it and realized that Charlie probably did know what he was talking about. He figured that if she didn't love him after she became a slut then she probably didn't love him that much to begin with. He knew that if he didn't try this, then he would probably stand a pretty good chance of losing her later on, whenever she got bored with him. Some oily encyclopedia salesman would come along and promise her the world and she would be gone. He had to find out now if she truly loved him or was she just following some script that she thought life was handing her.

"Your table's ready," a pretty waitress walked up to them, holding two menus to her breasts. She was an absolute knockout with her blonde hair and blue eyes. She was definitely the only girl in the place who could contest Julie's ability to turn heads.

Julie and Dave got up and followed her to their table. It was way over in the back in the smoking section. The fact that she had taken up smoking also turned him on. She was like the high school bad girl, or something.

After they were seated, Julie held up her menu and whispered to Dave.

"She is so gorgeous!"

Dave agreed.

"God, I wished I had legs like that."

Dave looked at Julie and smiled inwardly.

"Your legs are great. I wouldn't change them for anything."

Julie blushed. "You're so sweet. You're a liar, but you're sweet. I mean look at them, they just go right up to her ass." Julie could feel herself getting wet just by talking about the girl. She would have to watch her mouth.

A thought crossed Dave's mind and he quickly dismissed it. But then it came back. He wondered if he should try to draw her out a little. It was the perfect opportunity. He thought for a nanosecond and then opened his mouth.

"If I didn't know any better, I would think you have a crush on that girl."

Julie blushed a little bit more and smiled.

"I just think she's beautiful is all," she said, but left out the part about salivating at the thought of what the girl's pussy might taste like.

Dave nodded. She wasn't going to bite. She was going to keep it all to herself. That would be fine. He would just have to be very careful not let her know that he knew about her. Not that this would make him reveal anything. Charlie said that he had that all mapped out and for Dave not to ever come out and tell her about his part in this otherwise it would ruin it. Dave agreed and decided not to push it. Why mess up a good thing?

He didn't think this for long.

"But what would you think if I did?" Julie said.

Here was his chance.

"I don't know. I would think it was pretty neat, I guess."

Julie thought for a second.

"You know, I've heard about this thing called a ménage a trois.

Dave tried his hardest to keep from smiling. Charlie was right. While he had loved the old Julie, he absolutely adored the new one.

22

As time passed and her wedding day approached, and Julie became more turned out, she slowly became more and more adjusted to her newfound slut status. Sometimes, however, she would still experience guilt regarding Dave. No matter what she did, she still couldn't completely shake these feelings.

But one evening, as she was closing out the cash register, Julie suddenly had a revelation about her current sexual situation. All of a sudden, it became clear to her what was going on. Fucking was the same as masturbating as far as she was concerned. She didn't need to tell Dave everything, did she? He certainly didn't tell her whenever he yanked off. With this realization, she truly no longer had a problem with what she was doing. It was a very freeing experience and the knowledge left her elated. However, out in the parking lot, Charlie was reaching a conclusion about what to do about Julie. He was going to have to finish the job on her and soon. The deadline that was her wedding day was fast approaching and if he hadn't finished turning her out by then, Dave would never forgive him and he would just end up looking like some asshole who was trying to use some cockamamie elaborate plan to screw his best friend's girl. Yep, tonight was going to have to be the night. The night of the final turn out.

After she finished closing, she met Charlie out in the parking lot. This was in order for him to give her her ritual nightly ride around town. Sometimes they would go back to the barbeque joint for a gangbang, sometimes he would just drive around while she gave him head. Sometimes, they would just go back to his place and he would tie her up and let Ingrid take care of her. She was pretty satisfied, because she never knew what was coming next. And that cock of his! How could she ever tire of that thing? She just loved the taste of his cum. She felt like she could drink it by the gallon. But the more she thought about it, it wasn't just his cum, it was all cum. She was getting to be a cum junkie. She made Dave finish up every time now by cumming in her mouth. She was sure that he had definitely noticed the difference in her behavior by now, but as long as he was getting to cum in her mouth, she was sure he didn't mind.

When they got into the truck that night, Julie immediately started stroking Charlie through his pants. He got hard instantly.

"Do you want me to suck you?" She asked eagerly.

Against all his sexual instincts, Charlie pushed her hand away. "Nah…"

Disappointed, she pouted. What the hell did he mean by that? Here he had gone and gotten her addicted to his cock and now he was withholding it. He wasn't going to get away that easily. She went for the dick again.

"You're gonna give me that cock," she said.

He pushed her away again, this time a little harder. He was going to get blueballs from this. He knew it, but he had to finish the thing tonight.

"No, Julie, I don't feel like it tonight," he lied. He was aching for her to suck him off, but in order for him to get his desired effect, he couldn't let her get off so easily.

This time she huffed back over to her side of the truck.

"I'm so horny, though. I don't know why you won't let me suck you off."

Putting on his best actor's face, he said, "I don't know. Maybe I'm just not getting turned on by you anymore."

She looked at him like she could run through him.

"What do you mean, you're not turned on by me anymore? A lot of men would love to get what you're getting."

"Yeah, I suppose. I just don't think that you're slutty enough for me."

Her jaw dropped.

"I don't believe what you just said."

"Yeah," he continued. "I mean you act kind of slutty, but I think it's all just an act. It's just that you never do anything without me there making you do it. If you were a real slut, you would go out and be doing stuff on your own."

She shook her head in disbelief. She knew that all this was a lie. What about the swing party? There was a lot more to her than he knew, but still his condescension pissed her off royally.

"Well, you're wrong, buddy. You think I'm just play-acting here? Well, you've got a thing or two to learn about me. There's no acting here. You've turned this girl out. I crave fucking. I can't wait to suck pussy and cock. I thirst for cum. You'll see how wrong you are."

Charlie smiled. His little ruse had worked like a charm. "Show me."

Setting her jaw, she smiled a mischievous little smile. "Take me to the adult movie theater."

Inwardly, Charlie high-fived himself. He couldn't wait to call Dave.

23

Julie was so excited she couldn't stand it as they drove over to the old part of the city. It had once been a beautiful place but over the last couple of decades, it had fallen into disrepair and the only people who populated it were bums, cops and perverts. Naturally, it was also the location of the adult theater.

Charlie grinned to himself. This was it. He knew that now she was going to be turned out for good. She would be getting so much strange tonight that there would be no going back. Normal sex would never be enough for her. He would have done everything he had said he would do to her and more. She would be perfect for Dave.

As they traversed the darkening city streets, Charlie pulled over to a convenience store.

"What are you doing? I want to get fucked," Julie said impatiently.

"I've just stopping for some beer and cigarettes, baby. Don't worry. There's going to be plenty of dick left for you. It ain't like they're not making any more."

"I'm just so horny."

Charlie got out of his truck.

"You wait here. I'll be back in a minute."

"I want to get out," she whined.

"No, you sit here and masturbate. I want you to ready to go."

Julie smiled to herself. She could handle that. She immediately pulled her skirt up and started rubbing her pussy. She couldn't wait for all the strange hands to be pawing her and all the strange dicks to be fucking her. Hell, she probably wouldn't ever know any of these guys' names. She couldn't wait to show Charlie just how wrong he was about her. This really put her into high gear and she immediately had an orgasm. She knew there was plenty where that came from. Orgasms came so easy for her lately that she knew she was in no danger of running out.

Inside the store, Charlie walked to the back of the store, near the beer aisle. He looked over to his truck and when he was satisfied that Julie couldn't see him. He called Dave.

"Dave, she's ready."

"Are you saying…"

"She's gonna be fully turned out."

Dave took a deep breath. "So, what do I do now?"

Charlie laughed nervously. "You need to be at the adult theater and help me do it."

"But won't she be ashamed of herself when she sees me?"

"No, man, she needs you there to see that you still love her no matter how big of slut she's become."

"But won't it kill the mood when she sees me?"

Charlie thought for a minute.

"You still got your wrestling mask?"

24

By the time they reached the adult theater, Julie was almost salivating. She was so horny that she couldn't keep from grinding against her hand. This would be the final stage of her being turned out. Her only regret was that she hadn't done this sooner.

Charlie grinned. After stopping to make the quick call to Dave, he had almost run to his truck. He couldn't wait to get in on what was about to happen. Julie would be offered to every strange, horny pervert in the theater. This would by far be her most hardcore experience. He couldn't wait for Dave to see just what a great job he had done with her. Now, there would be no way that she could ever turn into the typical frigid housewife. In fact, Charlie almost pitied what Dave was going to get. There would be no way he could ever keep up with her. She would absolutely wear him out.

As they approached the old theater building, Julie began to get a little more excited.

"We're here," Julie said and started squirming. She was so turned on that her skin was hot to the touch. She was filled with an almost primitive feeling. It was like she was in heat or something, she thought. She was working on such a primal level that there was no way that she would be able to talk herself out of his. Not that she ever would have. Charlie was going to see a real slut tonight. This was one thing she vowed to herself.

Dave, on the other hand, was still at home, desperately trying to find his wrestling mask. It was imperative that he conceal his identity because he had to see how Julie was when she lost all her inhibitions. He had heard all the stories and now he wanted to see the results. He was so glad that Charlie had suggested this to him. Sure, he had the typical jealous feelings at first, but they had soon been replaced by feelings of arousal. It turned him on to no end to think of all the stuff she was doing. He couldn't wait to see it first hand, even if he was a little apprehensive of revealing himself to her.

All eyes were on Julie and Charlie as they walked into the run-down theater. The ticket guy leered at Julie as Charlie paid for them to go in. Charlie winked at him and smiled. The ticket guy smiled back. He had seen this a dozen times before. A guy brings his girl into the adult theater to let everybody there have a go at her. It was the ultimate slutty act. It just didn't get any better than this. Julie almost oozed she was so ready.

Julie was almost intoxicated with lust. She realized what her place in life was. It was to be a slut. It was to fuck and be fucked. It was to live life as sexually as possible. Sure she would have a job and a life, but it would always be underscored by sex. It would be just like the animal kingdom, except more honest. A lot of people would not like the way she was, but she didn't care. She wouldn't tell Dave, but if he found out, he would have to make a choice. She wasn't changing. Most people can't handle honesty especially when it deals with human need and desire.

They walked through the door into the darkened theater and no one noticed them at first. Everybody's gaze was fixed upon the naked woman and man having sex on the screen. Moans of self pleasure came from the audience and further served to drive Julie to the point of orgasm.

She and Charlie walked up to the front of the theater so that everyone's attention would be upon her. She immediately began to disrobe so that she was wearing nothing but her high heels. To get things started Charlie started feeling her up and kissing her neck. She eagerly got down on all knees and began sucking his cock. The mood of the audience began to change as their attention was diverted from the screen. As Julie sucked, everyone began to put their self-gratification in high gear.

After being sucked for a long slow time, Charlie bent Julie over a theater seat and began giving it to her doggie-style. Pretty soon, everybody in the theater got the hint and they started lining up. One in front and one behind. She had two lines, one for sucking and one for fucking. When the lines started forming, she came instantly. How many times she came after that, she didn't know. She lost count at ten. She didn't realize that it was possible for a person to be so turned on.

Julie couldn't believe the bliss she was feeling and the satisfaction she was giving herself. This was her at her most primitive. This was the way would have been back in the cave woman days. Sharing herself to anybody and everybody she pleased. She was finally sating her primal lust.

"Am I slutty enough, now, Charlie?" she asked defiantly and winked.

"I think slutty doesn't even describe you at this point," Charlie laughed.

Julie laughed too and got back to sucking.

Once the lines formed, Charlie stepped back and watched. He looked all over for Dave, but didn't see him anywhere. Finally, when he saw a guy wearing a wrestling mask enter, he knew it was him. He eagerly watched for his reaction which was hard to see because of the mask. At first the masked figure stopped. He seemed as though he just didn't know how to take all this. He seemed stunned. Charlie knew that his mind was being overloaded and that no preparation he could have given him could have been enough. Finally though, the figure started walking fast, breaking into a run towards Julie. At first, Charlie was afraid that Dave was going to start busting heads, but that wasn't the case. Instead he got into the blowjob line. He pushed his way to the front fast, pissing off several of the guys who were already on their second time around.

Julie smiled at him as she pulled his dick from his pants. "Oooh! A wrestler!"

She immediately went to work. She was getting it doggie-style and she continued with that without missing a beat. She went to work hard on him.

As Dave looked down at Julie he was just simply amazed. At first, those old feelings of jealousy had flooded him, but as just as rapidly, they disappeared. He was amazed. Here was his girl doing everybody in the world, and he was the man that she wanted to marry. She had experienced everything and he was still the man for her. He was just overwhelmed by his feelings.

Dave came quickly, further coating Julie's already cum-drenched face. She smiled at him as she licked her lips.

With that, he took off his mask.

Julie was shocked to say the least. "Dave!"

He just smiled at her as she turned a brilliant shade of red.

Charlie stood there keeping his fingers crossed.

25

As Julie and Dave left the church in their horse drawn carriage, they couldn't help but feel elated. Here they were, finally married and nothing but the rest of their lives in front of them.

Dave gave Julie a big kiss as they pulled into the main road. He just couldn't believe the love he felt for her. After he had finally revealed himself to her at the theater, she had been so embarrassed she wanted to go hide. She was so ashamed of herself that she said that she never wanted him to see her again. She grabbed her clothes and ran out of the theater. He chased her unrelentingly until he had finally caught up with her, about a block down the street. It had taken a lot of talking to convince her that he was happy that she had been turned out. He wouldn't have it any other way.

"Really?" she sniffled.

"Really," Dave said. He hugged her, not minding for a bit the fact that she was covered in other men's gism.

Of course Charlie had been following them and any thoughts that Dave had about keeping secret his role in the plan were soon blown.

"Dave and I planned the whole thing," he gasped. "We were in the Marines together, right, Dave?"

It was Dave's turn to turn red. He was extremely embarrassed at this revelation.

Julie turned to Dave.

"You mean that you...?"

"Let me explain," Dave started, but before he could go any further, she stopped him.

"You don't have to. I know I was a real prude."

"No you weren't," Dave corrected.

"Yes, I was. I was just so naïve and silly that I didn't have enough sense to know what I wanted."

"You weren't silly or naïve. You were just innocent."

Julie gave him a wry smile.

"Well, I'm not any more." She winked.

Dave turned red again while Charlie almost beamed with pride.

"Thanks to you and Charlie, I'm experiencing stuff I never even dreamed existed. I think if this could happen to every girl, there would be a lot more happy people. It just feels so good to do what you want whenever you want and with whomever you want. It's just one of the greatest feelings in the world."

Charlie waved his goodbyes, seeing that he had become a third wheel. When it was only she and Dave, she turned to him.

"Well, where do we go from here?"

"Well, we get married of course," Dave said.

"I know that. But I want to know about you. Do you think that you can handle all this?"

"What do you mean?" Dave was puzzled by the direction her conversation was taking.

Julie sighed and lit a cigarette.

"Well, I'll just tell you. I'm gonna keep doing this kind of stuff. I'm a slut and that's a door that I don't want shut again. It has to be this way. I love you with all my heart, but if you tried to stop me, I'll leave. I'll be sad, but I'll have to go."

Dave smiled and put his arms around her.

"You don't have to worry about a thing. I'm perfectly okay with all this. Above everything else, I want you to be happy. "

"But what if you have a problem with it later on? What then?"

Dave sighed.

"I'll just get over it. I know that I want you to be with me and if that is to happen I have to accept you as you are." He leaned over and kissed her. "And that is one thing that I definitely do."

She blushed.

By the time their wedding day rolled around a couple of months later, they were firmly comfortable with each other and all the activities that she engaged in. She was no longer embarrassed and he was no longer jealous. They both couldn't wait for her to get into action on the weekends. Everything was great. Dave got promoted right before the wedding and Julie graduated and was offered a job at the city library. While she missed Lucy, she did not miss the mall at all. Besides, Charlie had quit the security job right after that anyway and she still saw Lucy on the weekends. In fact, those two had even started going out together. After graduation, Josie left for Hollywood and to try her luck in the adult film business. She promised to get Julie in a film when she came out to visit. The Librarian opened up her own swing club in town and always let Julie and Dave in for free. She said that Julie really livened things up. Things always got a little wilder when she was around.

As the carriage took them to Dave's place, Julie couldn't help that life was pretty sweet. It was just too bad that she hadn't started this sooner.

Black Bra and Panties

1

Josie stepped out of the airport and into the bright California sunlight.

It felt so good to be back.

She adjusted the hem of her short skirt as she walked to the taxi stand. It seemed that it was always riding up and partially showing her bottom. It wasn't that she minded anyone seeing her bottom. It was just that it was a little uncomfortable. The way she looked at it, either she was wearing a skirt or she wasn't. If it kept riding it up, she would definitely have to just take it off. The only problem was that she wasn't wearing any panties. She didn't mind anyone seeing her like that either. She just didn't want to get arrested. She attracted attention with her gorgeous looks and dark red hair, but sometimes attention wasn't always a good thing. She had been arrested once before for public lewdness at a Lakers game, so she didn't want to go *there* again. She had been told by some unreliable sources that if she flashed the TV camera, it would boost her career in the adult industry. Of course, it hadn't. Her footage was never shown and all she ended up with was a fine.

Regardless, it was good to be back in Los Angeles. She had just spent a boring week at her parents' place back east and was ready to get back into the swing of things. It had been nice to visit home, and while she had felt great about being there, she felt even better about leaving. Of course, her parents had been all hung up about her career choice, even though they had always told her to "follow her dream." She couldn't help it that her dream just happened to be in porn.

While she had always been sexually promiscuous, it was only after her college roommate, Julie, had helped to turn her out that she realized that she wanted to be a porno actress. It was the first time she had been home since she had started making movies. The parental units were *not* very happy. Unlike most of the girls who hid their on-screen sexual activities from their parents, she had never had any hesitation about telling them. They had always said they would love her "no matter what." And they did, but they couldn't help but foster a bit of the typical parental judgmental behavior. They were such hypocrites, she thought. Her dad, Hal, was a motivational speaker and self-help guru. He was initially afraid that it would hurt his business, but had only reluctantly admitted that since she started screwing on film, his business had increased by forty-six percent.

He had said, "Josie, I know that you think it's cool and everything, but don't you ever think about where you'll be in five years?"

"Yes, Daddy, I have. I think that I'll still be in California making porno."

He shook his head. "What I'm saying, dear, is do you think that you'll want to do something else? Like maybe work in sales or be a nurse. Or even a lawyer."

She thought about this for a second. "I don't know. I mean, why would I want to do stuff like that? It's not like what I do is hard work or anything plus I make really good money."

Her father threw up his hands in desperation.

Her mother, Priscilla, a gorgeous middle-aged woman, was a little more receptive about her career choice.

"So, do you get to have threesomes and everything?" Priscilla asked.

Josie couldn't help but blush. "Mom! I can't believe you just asked me that!"

"C'mon. I just want to be supportive. So, do you get to have group sex?"

Josie rolled her eyes. "Yes, Mom. I get to have group sex. I basically do whatever it is they want me to do and if that includes group sex, I do it."

Mom leaned in close and looked over her shoulder to see if Dad was listening. He wasn't. He was busy trying to fix a clasp on Josie's bracelet. It had broken on the flight over.

"So, do a lot of the fellows have really big...you know?" Priscilla held out her hands to emphasize.

Josie blushed again. "Mom!"

"Tell me. I bet you really get it good, don't you?"

Josie sighed and smiled. She couldn't believe that her mom was being so cool with this. "Well, most of them are pretty big. But this one black guy had a dick that was…" Josie used her hands to illustrate a penis that was around ten inches long.

Her mom gasped in amazement.

"I'm so happy for you, honey. Doing what you want like this. I just wish I had had the guts to do what you do at your age. I mean it's taken me years…"

Before she could finish, Dad loudly cleared his throat and gave her a look.

She stopped what she was saying and quickly changed her tone. "Oh…I'm sorry. I'm happy that you're happy, but you really need to be careful. I would hate for you to get hurt."

Josie thought that it was a little odd that her mom had changed the subject like that, but thought no more of it. She spent the rest of her week hanging out at the house and seeing her old high school friends. Most of them were now either married or fat. These were the ones that hadn't gone away to college like her. Some of them were a little shocked at her career, but most seemed envious. Especially the male ones. They thought that it was amazing that she got paid to have sex on film. Josie didn't really pay them too much attention though, because they were all dumpy and had beerbellies.

Yes, it was boring. It hadn't been hard for her to come back to California.

The taxi pulled up at her apartment and she paid the cabbie and went in.

Her roommate, Marcy, was sitting on the sofa watching television. She was also a porno actress and was built like a brick shithouse. She had definitely gotten her money's worth when she had gotten her breast implants. Josie was still on the fence as far as breast augmentation went. Her fans begged her not to, but it seemed as though the industry people were hounding her to do it. She just didn't know what to do so she did nothing. She thought she had pretty good tits. She had never had any complaints about her C-cups.

As soon as she saw Josie, Marcy leaped up and hugged Josie.

"I'm so glad you're back! Did you have a good trip?" She gave Josie a deep open-mouthed welcome-home kiss. She and Josie, while not being lesbians or anything, occasionally had sex together when they were bored and horny and didn't feel like going out.

They did this stuff in the movies all the time, so why wouldn't they do it in real life, as well?

Josie returned the kiss and ran her hand between Marcy's legs, feeling her pussy lips through her tight black stretch pants.

"I'm glad to be back."

Marcy purred, "I couldn't wait for you to get back."

She began to nuzzle Josie's neck and put her hand up Josie's top, feeling her firm breasts. Josie responded by putting her hand in Marcy's pants. Marcy quickly worked her way down Josie's toned body with her tongue. Once she was on her knees, she pushed Josie's skirt up and began to kiss Josie's pussy. Josie moaned. It was the first time she had had sex since she had left California. She had left immediately after filming an eight man gangbang and had hoped that that would hold her until she got back. It hadn't.

Josie maneuvered Marcy over to the sofa so that the dark haired girl could access her pussy more easily. She loved having sex with Marcy. The girl knew exactly what buttons to push and she couldn't help but writhe and whip her red hair in ecstasy as the dark haired girl worked her pussy into a froth. Marcy worked like madwoman, eating like she was starved. Josie came twice before she couldn't even think about it.

"Are you going to let me have a taste?" She said breathlessly as Marcy continued to lap her up.

"Oh, yeah!" Marcy grinned as she looked up from between her legs.

Marcy climbed up on the couch and pulled down her pants and let Josie go to work, but not before deeply kissing Josie. Josie loved the taste of herself on Marcy's lips and got even more turned on as she got started. As she licked Marcy's big lips, she fingered herself to another orgasm. Marcy came almost immediately once Josie got started. The girls kept at it for a good hour before they finally were spent.

Laying there half-dressed and smoking cigarettes, Josie's attention wandered between Marcy and the TV.

"So, did your parents get on your nerves?" Marcy asked as she stroked Josie's leg.

"No, not really, just the usual what-am-I doing-with-my-life crap."

"What did you tell them?"

"Nothing much. I mean, what am I gonna say when they ask me what I'm going to be doing in five years when I don't know?" Josie said.

Marcy nodded.

Josie looked down and ashed her cigarette. What would she be doing in five years? Sure, being a porno actress was fine, but what about the other parts of her life? Surely, there was more to her than just sex? She tried to push these serious thoughts out of her head. She turned her attention to the television.

"Who's that?" She said as she looked at a wild looking red-haired man preaching fire and brimstone to a bunch of shabbily dressed parishioners. He looked to be in his mid-thirties and sported a big, slicked back pompadour and sideburns. He could have been a rockabilly singer just as easily as he was a fundamentalist preacher. His look gave off the impression that if he hadn't been a preacher he would have probably been in prison. He grinned maniacally as he stalked around the stage. They watched in amazement as he grabbed a slick haired man in an expensive suit from behind the organ. The guy didn't look surprised though. In fact, he looked like one of the preacher's right hand men. The preacher then proceeded to remove his own belt and tie it around the hands of the man.

"You've got to throw that devil out! Throw him out!"

With that, he grabbed the man, who was laughing, and threw him off stage. "Get out, Satan! Get out of my church!"

Then he turned to the congregation. "That devil won't be bothering us no more, brothers and sisters." He grinned and wiped his brow.

Then he went back to stalking around the stage and pounding his Bible.

The two girls looked on in amazement.

"I think that's Brother Red Hair," Marcy said. "I think that this show is called, *The Church of What's Happenin' Now.*"

"*What's Happenin' Now?* Man, he looks happenin' to be going crazy," Josie laughed.

"It must be the red hair," Marcy said winking. "You know what they say about those redheads."

Josie stared at her in mock anger.

"I'm gonna get you for that!" With that she pounced on Marcy and the two girls started up again.

2

As he relaxed in his recliner and got a blowjob, Brother Leon "Red" Hair smoked a cigarette and realized that he was, by far, the luckiest person he had ever known. And this was saying something, because he had met quite a few people. He had grown up in a little town in Texas, impoverished and with no apparent prospects. Everybody there had considered him to be typical local white trash. They figured he would either end up in a factory or in prison, just like ninety percent of the rest of the town's population.

However, there was one thing that they didn't know about Red. That was the fact that he had dreams. Sure, this didn't make him any different from any of the other assholes who lived in the town. Most of them had dreams too. Their dreams were the typical mundane small town fantasies of being rich, having a nice car, joining the Army or getting married. However, his were a little more specific.

He had at first wanted to be a science fiction writer. He had an idea for a masterpiece titled, *The Man Who Could Shit Worlds*. He wasn't sure if he would ever be able to put the astounding concepts in his head down on paper but he would try. The book would be about a man who through some amazing mental evolution could actually defecate galaxies. The whole concept of everything in the world being nothing but the waste material of a greater organism was a riveting one for Red. The novel would be mind boggling, but only if he could organize his thoughts enough to write it. It would be his life's crowning achievement. And if that didn't work out, he wanted to be a TV preacher.

Most people just couldn't see that Red was different from all the rest of the losers in town who claimed to have dreams. The difference was that he knew how to make his come true. Since he had chronic writers block and had never been able to write the first sentence of his magnum opus, he had opted for the latter dream. The one about being a TV preacher.

He moved the girl's head up and down on his penis with his heavily tattooed arms, a byproduct of a brief rebellious streak in his early twenties. The tattoos were of Biblical scenes such as the burning bush and Judas hanging himself. He sometimes used them as tools to better illustrate his sermons. With their bright colors and amazing detail, they looked absolutely stunning on TV.

One of Red's most important characteristics was that in addition to loving church and to study people, he also hated to see people suffer. Since he had grown up poor, he was always looking for a way to help out the underprivileged. He knew that being a preacher would be a good way to do this. While he was a true believer, he also realized early on that no matter what kind of nonsense passed through the lips of the most religious people in the congregation, it would inevitably be accepted as fact. It did not matter out outrageous or tongue in cheek it was, as long as it was presented with a lot of fire and brimstone, shouting and pew-jumping, people would believe it. One of the deacons could come in one day and say something to the order of, "Man didn't walk on the moon. It was all a trick of the devil to make everybody lose sight of God." Sure enough, five minutes later, everybody in the congregation would accept as truth the fact that man didn't walk on the moon, whether they actually believed it or not. They were afraid to say anything in opposition to it for fear of being labeled an atheist.

Red made note of all this and realized that he could pretty much go out there and say anything he wanted. And as long he kept it within the context of religion and gave the people the show they expected, he would always be able to find someone to follow him. But moreover, he could use this power to help people. People are always more likely to help others if there is religion involved. He always considered himself a good person and hated to see people in misery. It was the perfect mix. Besides, he was good looking and charismatic. That didn't hurt either.

Another thing going for him was the fact that he had always been popular with the girls in church. The funny thing about it was that while he was considered to be a very handsome boy, none of the girls ever really paid any attention to him until one day he started nodding off in church. He had stayed up late the night before watching *The Good, The Bad and the Ugly*, and could barely keep his eyes open. Of course when he started falling asleep, he started to get really relaxed and before long, he had a boner the size of Houston in his pants. He had always considered it a blessing that he was so well-endowed, but still he didn't think he was anything special. After all, eleven inches wasn't that big, was it?

The girls really started eyeing him and making every effort to get him to go home with them. He did, of course, and lost his virginity very quickly. He bedded every girl in his Sunday school class within the month, but only after they had had a private Bible study. He soon came to see his prodigious penis as a divine tool. The sessions kept up pretty regularly and news of the size of his penis eventually got around to the older, married women in the church as well. Soon, he was also being invited over for *private* Bible studies with them.

But of all the women in the congregation with whom he had sex, his favorite was the preacher's wife. She was about thirty-five years old and was built for sex. She had no children and her body was tight from working out five times a week. Her large natural breasts begged to be sucked and her perfect ass begged to be fucked.

The first time they met, she invited him over for fried chicken. He had already been through this scenario several times with some of the other women so he was already hard before they even started eating the chicken. He couldn't keep his eyes off her breasts. She was squeezed into a too-tight sundress and the big babies were about to pop out. He ached to get his hands on her. She, on the other hand, could see the thick bulge through his pants and couldn't wait to get her lips around that thing. But they couldn't just launch themselves at each other too quickly. After all, she had gone to a lot of trouble to cook the chicken. And besides, they were having homemade ice cream for dessert.

"So, I guess the Reverend isn't coming back for a while?" Red said as he bit into a chicken leg. He was already drooling at the prospect of licking the preacher's wife's pussy. The chicken was a poor substitute, even though it was extremely good.

"He's going to be gone all day. He's had to check out some new hymnals," she said, crossed her legs and took a bite of fried okra.

Red finished his leg and cleared his throat.

"Could I have a breast please," he said and smiled. He looked directly at her breasts.

"Um…yeah. Anything you want. Just ask," she said and picked up the bowl of chicken and leaned over to him brushing her breasts against his face. He couldn't control himself and took a nibble through her dress as she leaned into him. She moaned a little and went back to her seat.

Red took a bite out of the chicken breast. "This is good."

The preacher's wife rubbed her pussy a little bit as she watched him eat.

"Uh huh."

After a couple more moments, she noticed that his glass was empty.

"Let me get you some more sweet tea, Red."

"I would like that," he said and rubbed her ass a little as she walked past him to the refrigerator.

She brought the pitcher back to the table and poured a little sweet tea, but couldn't help but splash a little on his lap.

"Oops," she said.

"That's ok," Red said. "It's only sweet tea."

"Oh, no it's not ok. I'm gonna have to clean that up."

"Ok," Red said.

With that, the preacher's wife got down on her knees and began to lick up the sweet tea from the front of his pants. Red's hard-on kicked into high gear. She unzipped his pants and before it even had a chance to stop bouncing, she started sucking him off. After a few strokes, she deepthroated him. All eleven inches. He was amazed. It was the first time anyone had ever deepthroated him completely. He knew that he was definitely staying for dessert.

After she sucked him almost to the point of ejaculation, she pulled up her dress and climbed up on the table. She spread her legs and pulled his face down to her pussy. She wasn't wearing any panties and she was so wet that she was dripping. Red loved eating pussy and he dove in with wild abandon, licking and sucking her clit. She pulled his head in close and hunched his face until she had an orgasm.

After that, she changed position and leaned over the table.

"Fuck me doggie style, church boy. I want to see how deep that big dick of yours can go."

Red stuck it in so fast that it took her breath away. He immediately started pounding her with everything he had. The dishes shook on the table and at one point, the chicken was in danger of falling onto the floor. The preacher's wife had reflex enough to grab it before it did though.

"Fuck me harder!" She ordered him.

He complied, pumping her with everything he had.

She came four twice before he breathlessly told her that he was about to cum.

"I want you to shoot it in my mouth," she said and pulled him out of her and got down on her knees and began to deepthroat him until he shot his whole load down her throat. After he finished, she swallowed and took a sip of sweet tea.

"Now, let's get back to our chicken."

Over the course of the rest of the meal, Red learned that the preacher was impotent and didn't mind for her to go around screwing other men. Just so long as they weren't in the congregation. That was one of his biggest rules. No one from the congregation.

Just after they finished their ice cream, to their chagrin, the preacher walked in, carrying a box of new hymnals. He took one look at them, sitting there in the nude and the hymnals dropped to the floor.

"Damn it! June! I told you not to fuck anybody from the church!"

"It's ok, Grover. He's a good boy and he's got a big…heart. He won't say nothing." She looked at Red. "Will you, Red?"

Red thought about it for a minute. This was the chance he had been waiting for.

"I won't say anything on one condition."

Both the preacher and the preacher's wife looked at each other and then looked at him with a great amount of consternation.

"How much do you want?" The preacher sighed.

Red smiled. "I don't want any money. I just want you to let me start preaching."

At that the preacher and his wife looked at each other with a look of befuddlement. Suddenly, the preacher started smiling.

"That's the best blackmail I've ever paid, boy. You've got yourself a deal."

The preacher's wife reached over and rubbed Red's penis.

"He loves it when he gets to mentor another preacher."

And so he got started. His relationship with the preacher and his wife got even closer, with him coming over several times a week to service her and for the preacher to give him tips on how to deliver effective sermons.

After graduating from high school, he started preaching wherever he could. His sermons were the typical fire and brimstone but soon, due to his young age and enthusiasm, he developed quite a following, especially among the homeless and downtrodden. These were people who always touched his heart, especially because they were so easy to manipulate. He soon figured out that if he gave them food and clothing, they would do pretty much anything he wanted.

The girls were no exception. One of his favorite things was to take a scruffy young woman, clean her up and take her back to his place for a *laying on of hands*. He would cure her of her ailments and give her a job. Then she would become a part of his inner circle for a while and provide him with the services he couldn't receive from any of his male co-workers. This would go on until he found another girl to help. He didn't want to deny any of them.

Because of his predilection for the homeless, he called his church the *Cardboard Cathedral*. However, he referred to his ministry as a whole as *The Church of What's Happenin' Now* partially to pay tribute to the Reverend Leroy, a television minister who had greatly influenced him as a young boy but also called it that to stress the immediacy of his message. He wanted everyone to know that his church was not about the past, and not about what people had done in their past, but rather what they were doing now and what they were going to do in the future. It was a message of forgiveness and inclusion.

He ran thrift stores and missions. He gave the homeless jobs. He gave them food and clothing and they gave him loyalty. Rapidly he expanded his empire. Eventually, he was able to buy a small TV station and from that he was able to realize his dream of starting his own cable network. He had everything a man could want. He advised several heads of state on spiritual matters and he could get any woman he wanted. But now he was finding himself becoming bored. He really felt as though he had done all there was to do as far as being a TV preacher went. He was jaded and blasé. Sitting there in the recliner with the girl's mouth on his dick made it all too clear to him.

"That's good, baby," he said as he shot his load into the girl's mouth.

She licked her lips and cleaned him off.

"Do you want me to do anything else, Brother Red?" She said sweetly.

"No, that's ok, Sister Gwen. Just go back and make sure that there are plenty of mattresses in the mission."

She smiled and left the room.

Naturally, Red's dalliance with the ladies of the church had shaped his attitudes about sex. Unlike a lot of the other religious people he knew, he didn't have any hang-ups and misconceptions about it. To him it was a great thing. It was about having fun and giving others pleasure.

Some people would have thought that his viewpoints on sex were a little too open-minded for a man of the cloth and he would have to say that he didn't blame them. Not everyone saw sex the way he did. In fact, he saw sex between consenting adults as completely natural and healthy. It was no moral gray area in his book. The trouble was, he couldn't come out and say this to anyone. He hated that he had to be this way. He felt dishonest about keeping his attitudes towards sex secret. However, he knew that if he came out and started preaching free love and whatnot that he would be completely alienated from his congregation and he could possibly lose his church. But on the other hand, he realized that he would probably also help a lot of people by letting them know that they weren't reprobates and perverts because they enjoyed a good threesome every now and again. He was constantly at battle with himself over this. However, he always took the path of least resistance and kept it secret. He figured that the good he did by keeping his mainstream congregation far outweighed what he would achieve if he came out and said that fucking was okay.

Red flicked on the TV and DVD player. He pressed play. He had been watching and re-watching the same porno movie for the last month or so. It was a nasty little film called *Black Bra and Panties* and starred a girl named Josie Bistro. In it, she went around trying to figure out where she had lost her expensive black bra and panties. Since she was quite an active girl, she was having a real problem tracking her belongings down. Also, she kept getting sidetracked by all the sex she kept getting involved in. He was so intrigued that he just couldn't stop watching it.

Actually, there was a little more to it than that, he thought that the girl was his destiny. Long ago, when he had first started out in the ministry he had started having a recurring dream about being married. Aside from the church, he never experienced such happiness as he did while he was having it. The dream was always the same. He was at a party and was looking everywhere for his wife. He wasn't panicked, but excited about finding her. He searched all over the house until finally he heard her voice. She was out in the backyard. He walked outside and saw her. She was down on all fours and surrounded by naked men. She was sucking everything that was presented to her and getting fucked by everyone. She was half-wearing a black bra and her black panties were hanging on the heel of her pump. He was so happy in this dream. His wife was beautiful, red-haired and was an absolute slut. When he had first seen *Black Bra and Panties*, he had almost fainted. The girl of his dreams was Josie.

It was fate. But how could he ever meet her? He was a famous televangelist and she was a porno actress. How could you make something like that work?

As the movie played and he watched her take it from a couple of meatheads, a light went off in his head.

He snapped his fingers and picked up the phone.

3

"Get it, Girl! Get it!"

Josie sucked the big black cock with even more abandon. The urging of the director wasn't even a factor in her performance. Between the cock in her mouth and the one dogging her from behind, she could barely pay attention to a word he was saying. After all, it wasn't every day that she was sucking the cock of Cedric Gunn and getting fucked silly by Jerome Crank. These two were legends in the industry. They were favorites of most of the porn girls due to their size and skill and here she was doing both of them at the same time!

Josie had dutifully reported to the set the day after she had gotten back in town. It was a rented house in a quiet, upscale residential area. Most of the neighbors were completely unaware that a porno movie was being shot there. While there were a few cars parked in the driveway, it looked more like the house was being shown to prospective buyers rather than it did a den of iniquity. The only giveaway was the abundance of large breasted, scantily clad women cavorting around.

She took a glance around her as she deepthroated the thick nine-incher. Other porno girls and guys lounged around reading magazines and talking to the crew and each other. Some were nude and some weren't. She was glad to be working. She sympathized with the actors because she always got bored when she waited around for her scenes to begin. At least it was her turn to work. But even more than that, she was glad to be fucking.

The nubian behind her pounded her like she had never been pounded before. He was by far the most aggressive partner she had ever had. He was literally pumping the orgasms out of her. She had at least three without even trying. One of him would have been enough for any girl, along with the massive penis in front of her, she thought she had died and gone to big cock heaven.

The director could barely contain himself as he jumped around giving them instructions.

"Now switch! I want to see that one there fuck her."

The two studs switched around and Josie was eager to get filled up with dick again. This time she lay on her back and got it missionary style while she leaned over and slurped on the big black cock.

"Suck it, girl," Jerome moaned as she licked the head of his dick. She could taste herself on him and she began to look longingly over at the naked girls sitting around awaiting their scenes. This made her suck even harder.

If she had thought the other guy fucked hard, he was nothing compared to this one. He was like a wild man. While the other guy pumped the orgasms out of her, this one was literally jarring them loose.

"Don't stop! Don't stop!" She said as she came for the third time that scene.

The stud fucking her just grinned and picked up the pace.

Eventually, the director signaled for the guys to cum and both disengaged themselves from her and masturbated themselves into her mouth. She eagerly lapped up the cum and cleaned their penises off. When the cameraman got in close to get a good shot of the cum on her face, she couldn't resist winking at the camera.

"You missed some," Cedric said and pointed to his dick. She smiled at the camera and licked up what she had missed.

The director was absolutely beaming after the scene.

"I think I'm gonna have go to jerk off now," he said and slapped the guys on the back. He winked at Josie and she playfully went after his crotch. She wasn't serious though because he was happily married to a woman who knew absolutely nothing about what he did for a living. Most of the other girls also tried to stay clear of him because they didn't want all the hassle that would ensue if his wife ever found out about him, But still, he had a way of working his charm with some of the younger girls. Josie couldn't help but roll her eyes as a fairly new young starlet followed him into the bathroom. She went to another part of the house and took a shower.

After she finished cleaning herself up, she put on a tight t-shirt and cutoff jeans and went to the kitchen. The two black guys were already in there eating some catered lasagna.

"Girl, you were absolutely fan-fucking-tastic," Cedric said as he chewed his lasagna.

"Well, let me tell you, when a girl gets fucked like that, she doesn't have a choice but to be fan-fucking-tastic," Josie laughed.

Jerome and Cedric laughed.

"You two finished for the day?" Josie asked.

At that, a pretty Latina walked up.

"This one had better not be finished, we've still got a scene," she said grabbing onto Jerome's dick though his pants. Jerome was instantly hard. She then playfully punched Josie on the arm. "I hope you didn't use up all his juice."

Josie playfully punched her back.

"Carmen, from the looks of him, I think there's plenty left to go around."

Jerome's pants now looked like a tent trying to open. He cracked up laughing.

"What about you, Josie? You got any more scenes?" He asked.

"I think me and miss thing here has one later." She winked at Carmen who leaned in and began to feel her up starting at her tits.

"You girls, keep that shit up, I'm gonna have to let this dog out!" Jerome said and pointed to his about-to-burst pants.

"Me too," Cedric said.

Carmen and Josie collapsed into giggles. Cedric and Jerome were probably the funniest two guys in porn. If they hadn't been so well-endowed, they could've probably become comedians, Josie thought. Not to say that comedians weren't well-endowed, but most of the ones that Josie had screwed had been hung like buttons.

"I don't think I'm gonna be able to wait for my scene. I'm gonna have to have me a taste right now," Carmen said and got down on her knees and extricated Jerome's cock from his pants.

While Carmen sucked, Josie grabbed a paper plate and started to serve herself some lasagna when all of sudden the director came running into the kitchen.

"Get your clothes on! Someone's outside!"

"Is it a cop?" Jerome said and continued to eat his lasagna.

"I don't know!" The director whined. "I can't go to jail. My wife will kill me!"

"You have a permit, don't you?" Carmen asked nonchalantly as she reluctantly let go of Jerome's dick.

"A permit! I didn't know I had to have a permit." Suddenly he grabbed Josie. "Here, you look innocent. Go answer the door."

Josie looked at him in shock. She didn't relish the thought of going to jail either. She didn't think shooting a porno was illegal, but she didn't want to find out the hard way that it wasn't.

"What about her?" Josie said and pointed to Carmen.

"No, she looks like a slut. It's got to be you. You look like somebody's daughter."

Jerome and Cedric winced at the comment and Carmen looked like she was ready to punch him.

"Shouldn't we go out the back?" Josie asked.

"No!" He shrieked. "If it's the cops, they'll be back there. Just go answer the door and tell them that we're having..."

"An Amway party?" Cedric suggested.

"Yes, an Amway party! Tell them we're having an Amway party!"

"What if I don't want to?" Josie countered.

"Do you want to work in the business again?"

"Man, that shit's cold," Cedric said under his breath.

"I'm serious. Do it or you're blacklisted." The director was almost foaming at the mouth at this point. His eyes were bugged out and he looked on the verge of losing it. "You won't fuck on film again."

"Oh, ok, then, I'll do it."

Reluctantly, Josie went to the front door. She noticed that the other actors had hastily dressed themselves and were sitting around with the crew like they were in church or something.

She opened the door, fully expecting to see a cop. She was a little surprised at what she saw.

It was an old slick haired guy and a sexy young woman and they were both carrying Bibles. While appearing to be clean, the old guy had the stench of poverty and homelessness. He was weatherbeaten from spending too much time outside and his suit was cheap, like it had been donated by somebody. The girl on the other hand, looked like a model or something and was dressed in a smart navy blue business suit. They were definitely the odd couple.

"Can I help you?" Josie asked.

The old man smiled.

"Sister, if you have a minute, I can tell you something that will change your life."

4

Getting ready for a swing party was always a big event at Josie's parent's house. Yes, there was at least one thing about her parents that Josie didn't know.

"Do I look ridiculous, honey?" Hal asked as he put on an enormous purple fur hat.

"You look great, dear," Priscilla answered as she sat on the bed fastening the strap on her six inch heel.

"I mean I really look like a pimp, don't I?" Hal said as he continued to survey himself in the bedroom mirror. The Pimps and Hookers Ball was only a once a year thing at their swing club and it was absolutely imperative for Hal to look his best. He was trying to maximize his potential and seize the moment and accomplish every other self-actualizing objective that he talked about in his seminars. Hal Bistro was definitely a man who practiced what he preached. However, he couldn't actually tell Priscilla that this was what he was doing because she hated for him to talk about his job. It bored her to tears.

"Well, I would definitely be your ho," Priscilla purred as she sidled up to Hal and started to stroke his penis through his pants.

"You're gonna have to slow down, baby. You don't want to waste it all on me. You can have me any time."

"I think I've got plenty to go around," she said and got down on her knees and took his penis out of his pink velvet pants.

"Well, I don't know if I do...oooh yeah, baby. Suck it just right that." He placed his hands on the back of her head and rubbed it as she deepthroated him. Up and down, up and down, he knew that she was going for it, so he might as well go along for the ride.

Priscilla pushed her short skirt up and began to rub her pussy. Hal could see that it was already wet. It was dripping and glistening and the sight of it made him that much harder. Occasionally she licked the hand she was rubbing her pussy with and sometimes she pushed it into Hal's mouth. After a few minutes, he heard her breathing quicken a little and she started to suck just a little harder. She was going to cum. A couple of seconds later, he could feel her body shudder and he was unable to hold it in any longer. He began to squirt his cum deep down into her throat. She looked him square in the eyes and gulped it like she was drinking a milkshake. Not one drop was wasted. She took the whole load. There would be no mess to clean up tonight. Not that there ever was.

Hal chuckled and gave her a kiss as she got to her feet. "Not bad for a couple of forty-year olds."

Priscilla lit a cigarette. "God, if I was as horny when I was in my twenties as I am now, I think I would have stayed pregnant."

The two of them finished dressing and went downstairs. Hal definitely looked the part in his purple hat and pink velvet suit. He had bought the outfit six months earlier at a yard sale. He had been chomping at the bit for this night. Priscilla would look hot wearing a burlap sack, but in her slutty, tight black dress and classic pumps, she looked good enough to eat.

After they got downstairs, Hal looked at his watch. "Well, it looks like we made it with time to spare."

"Wow, we've got a whole ten minutes. Do you want me to fix you a drink before Bob and Jenny show up?" Bob and Jenny were an over-tanned, oily but good looking couple around the same age as Hal and Priscilla. The two couples swung fairly regularly and considered each other to be good friends. They also played golf together occasionally.

"Only if you're fixing yourself one."

"Well, I am. I want to get a little bit loosened up for this thing. You know I've been a little distracted what with Josie not being here and all."

"I know, dear. You just like to worry."

"I know. I just don't like her being all the way out there in California by herself."

She walked over to the bar and began to fix two martinis. "Don't think it's about time that we told her about us?" She said as she took the vodka from the freezer. "After all, she is a porno actress. I think she'll be able to handle it."

Hal shook his head. "We've been over this before, Pris. I just don't think it's a good idea. You know part of the reason that she's in porn is to rebel against us. Can you imagine what it would do to her if she found out that we're probably more sexually active than she is? It would really upset her world."

"You're probably right," Priscilla said as she poured the vermouth. "She might think she's got to go to even greater extremes to shock us. She might start using drugs."

"Or she might become a religious fanatic," Hal said.

"I don't know what I would do if that happened. I shudder to think of it."

"Well, maybe it wouldn't be so bad."

"Then again, maybe it would," she said.

Priscilla brought the drinks over and they began to sip. Hal lit a cigarette.

"You know, I can't help but be a little jealous of her. She's really got her priorities straight at such a young age."

Hal took a big sip. "Yeah, she's got her priorities straight, but I just wish she would be a little more concerned about her future.

She can have just as much sex being a banker or a lawyer as she can being a porno actress."

"She's young. She just doesn't realize it."

Just then, the doorbell rang.

"They're here." Priscilla quickly downed her drink and went over and opened the door.

"Hey, swingers!" Bob said, swinging a big black walking stick and sporting a lavender polyester leisure suit. His platform shoes made him a full five inches taller than Jenny who was dressed in a tight red tube dress and go-go boots with six-inch heels. Bob looked like a pimp, sure enough, but he was definitely not pimp enough to out-pimp Hal.

"What up, pimp!" Hal said as he finished his drink. "Do you two want one?"

"No, we're fine," Jenny said.

"I had my drink before you two came over," Priscilla said and winked.

They all started laughing and walked to the minivan. Hal and Priscilla couldn't wait to see who was going to be at the party. They weren't going to worry any more about telling Josie their dirty little secret. It could wait until later. They had plenty of time.

5

Josie parked her Nissan on the sun drenched, tree lined street and walked the short distance to Gunter Bumsen's house. A guy washing his car dropped the hose when he saw her in her lowcut jeans and halter top. She was definitely smoking today. However, sex was not on her mind. She was here to see Gunter. Gunter was a German porn actor with whom Josie had had the pleasure to work on several occasions. Over in Europe, he was almost mainstream. He was always being asked to appear at openings of sex shops, book stores and shopping malls. Over here, he was just another porno actor. He was typically full of bullshit, saying that he split his time between the states and Europe because he just couldn't stand the celebrity at times. Of course, he also complained that people in the states didn't have enough of an appreciation for him. His ego wouldn't let him see that while he was a muscular, somewhat good looking guy, he was still just a porno actor. His euro-mullet didn't help his cause much either.

While Josie had always enjoyed working with him because he had a large penis and really knew how to fuck, she wasn't here today to discuss business. She was here to talk about the metaphysical. He was a self-styled mystical type and, for some reason, when it came to spiritual matters, all the porno types always looked to him for advice. Apparently none of them had ever caught on to the fact that he didn't know anything.

After the appearance of the weird old guy and gorgeous girl at the porno shoot, Josie had been thrown for a loop. She had taken the old guy up on his assertion that he could change her life and had allowed him into the house. Of course, the director immediately threw them out so they had to talk in the driveway.

At first, Josie had begun to feel a little guilty about doing porno when she was confronted with the idea of talking to a religious person. But the old man shook his head at such thoughts. He also couldn't help but drool at the sight of Josie in her tight t-shirt and cutoff jeans.

"What would you say if I told you it doesn't matter what you do or what you've done. What would you say if I told you that you are accepted, no matter what?"

"Unless you've killed somebody, of course," the pretty girl, who had introduced herself as Sister Gwen, added. "You haven't killed anybody, have you?"

"Um…no. I still don't understand what you've talking about," Josie said.

The old man, whose name was Brother Farlin, lit up a cigarette. "We're talking about Brother Red Hair and his Cardboard Cathedral. You know, *The Church of What's Happenin' Now*. We want you and your friends to come down and sit in on a service. We want you to come on down and see what we're all about."

"But why? We're just porno people. I would've thought that someone like Brother Red Hair would hate us."

The pretty girl started smiling and shook her head.

"Oh, no. Brother Red may preach fire and brimstone, but he doesn't have anything against people who work in the sex industry. He thinks it's a shame that you're so ostracized when you have so much to offer."

Josie couldn't help but notice that the girl was checking her out.

"Heck, I used to be a prostitute before I started to going to the Cardboard Cathedral," Sister Gwen said.

"And he didn't care?" Josie asked incredulously.

"Heck no. He said come on in. We need some more whores!" she laughed.

Brother Farlin nodded his head, not once taking his eyes off Josie's breasts.

"Well, I'll think about going some time then," Josie said to get them to move along.

Sister Gwen and Brother Farlin beamed at each other.

"One thing though," the girl said. "All new girls have to wear black bras and panties. It's very symbolic to Brother Hair. He insists on it."

"That's kind of odd, but I guess if it's symbolic..." Josie said. She paused for a second. "You know? I did a movie about black underwear once."

"Really?" Sister Gwen said and uncomfortably cleared her throat. She then pulled her shirt down to show Josie her own black bra. She smiled. "I always wear mine."

After shaking hands and telling her how much they looked forward to seeing her in church, the two then handed Josie some pamphlets and tract literature and walked off. Josie went back into the house and did her scene.

Usually, this sort of thing didn't affect her. The whole religion thing. However, for some reason, she just couldn't get her mind around it. She had read and re-read the tracts which were mostly concerned with how everyone was going to hell. They also stressed the importance of tithing and how you should help your fellow man.

No, it wasn't the tracts. It also wasn't the fact that she kept seeing Brother Red Hair on the TV every time she turned it on.

It was the comment about the black bra and panties. That was what had her puzzled. What the hell did that mean? When she had told Marcy about it, she had suggested that she go see Gunter.

"If anybody will know, he will," Marcy said.

So, that's what she was doing.

"Hallo, Baby," Gunter said as he opened the door.

"Hello, Gunter," she said and kissed him on his cheeks in the European fashion to which he was accustomed. She also overlooked the annoying fact that he referred to everyone, male and female alike as "baby." For some reason, when he had learned English, he had gotten the idea that this was a cool thing to do and no one had ever had the heart to tell him differently.

They went into the living room and sat down. A couple of girls were sitting on the floor with their legs crossed meditating. Josie pointed to them as if to ask if they would be disturbing them.

"Oh, no, baby. They are so high, they still they think they are in Belgium!" He laughed.

They had a seat on a large beanbag sofa. On the coffee table in front of them sat a very new deck of Tarot cards. These were strictly for show, because Gunter had no clue as how to read them. If asked to give a reading, he would always say something to the effect that he had a spiritual blockage and would be unable to do it accurately. He would defer to his magic eight ball instead.

"So, baby, what can I help you with?"

Josie explained what was going on. Gunter nodded and gestured in a way that suggested that he understood exactly what she was talking about.

"Marcy said that if anybody would know, you would."

Gunter pondered for a moment, visibly turning it over in his mind.

"While I have devoted my life to studying the great mysteries, I have to admit that this is quite unusual."

"Yes?"

"Let me pause to think for a moment, baby. I have to try to channel the power of the ancients to discover the answer to the riddle that you seek."

At that he closed his eyes and started chanting. To Josie, he sounded like he was reading off the periodic chart or something. She didn't say anything, though. He was supposed to be "at one" with things.

After a few minutes, he suddenly smiled and opened his eyes. "I think I have your answer. I was able to channel the spirit of an ancient medicine man. He gave me the answer you seek."

Josie's eyes opened wide.

"What is it? What does it mean?" She asked excitedly.

Gunter smiled even more widely.

"The medicine man thinks that maybe this preacher just likes black bras and panties, baby."

Josie looked at him incredulously. Was that it? Was that the opinion of a man who was supposedly spiritually in tune?

Gunter leaned back and smiled.

"So, baby, now that I've answered your question, do you want to screw now?"

Josie hadn't really thought about it, but she was feeling a little horny.

"Sure, why not?" She said and took off her skirt.

Gunter was hard instantly and Josie was down on her knees worshipping his cock within seconds. The two stoned girls just looked on with a vague detachment. It was like they were watching television or something.

Josie went to work on his cock like a pro. He was muttering in German and the pre-cum came up fast. Josie fingered herself as she blew him, occasionally tasting herself.

Her head bobbed up and down like a machine as she brought up his cum.

"You better slow down, baby. I'm not going to get to fuck you if you keep that up," Gunter said, slowing her head down.

"Well, let's just get down to the fucking then," Josie said matter of factly and crawled up into his lap, putting his dick in her pussy with one fluid movement.

"Let's do it this way," Josie said as she started to grind against him.

Gunter's eyes rolled to the back of his head as she flexed her vaginal muscles around his big dick. She rode him like a mechanical bull, except she was in no danger of getting thrown.

"Ugh, I love your big cock," Josie moaned and quickened her pace. She sped up to the point where their skin was making slapping noises as they went together. She groaned as she crescendoed into a massive orgasm. Gunter struggled to hold on and was relieved when she finally came.

"Where do you want it, baby?" Gunter said breathlessly.

"Cum in my pussy," she said.

At that, Gunter squirted a massive load deep inside of her. She started shuddering again as he pumped her full. She was having another orgasm.

After they were finished, Josie put her clothes on and resolved that she had to start going to church.

6

"Brothers and sisters! Are you ready! Are you down with What's Happenin' Now? Are you up with what's happenin' today?" A big black guy in an expensive light blue suit smiled broadly as he stood on the stage of the Cardboard Cathedral. The congregation exploded into amens and hallelujahs.

At that the big Hammond organ at the back of the stage started playing the most rocked out and boogie woogied up gospel music that Josie had ever heard. The drums joined in and the big black guy started clapping his hands. The congregation followed suit. "Amen, brothers and sisters!"

The guy at the organ, the slick haired guy who Josie had seen being tied up and thrown off the stage on television, was going crazy playing the organ. He was like some sort of Pentecostal Liberace or something.

"And here he is, brothers and sisters, Brother Red Hair!" The big black guy stepped to the side as Brother Red Hair walked very fast out to the stage. He was all smiles and was already sweating. He wore an expensive tan suit and a very stylish scarlet tie.

"Thank you, Brother Abernathy," Red said to the big black guy.

"Hallelujah!"

"Hallelujah!" Red answered back.

The organ music died down and the church grew quiet.

"Brother Myrtlewood is revved up on that organ, ain't he bruthas and sistas?"

Brother Myrtlewood Green beamed at the recognition by Red.

Red surveyed the congregation and was extremely proud of what he was seeing. He was amazed every time he preached to such a big crowd. There was so much love out there that it overwhelmed him. He was determined that this was going to be one his best sermons ever. He knew that his very special lady was out there somewhere and he had to make it count. He was so psyched he could barely stand still.

After Red began his sermon, he began to run around the stage like a madman. He preached and hollered, always eliciting a chorus of "Amen, Brother!" or other sayings like that. Occasionally people would simply raise their hands up and wave them in the air.

Josie sat up in the farthest reaches of the building, spellbound by what she was seeing. She had never seen a religious sermon like this. She had grown up an Episcopalian and was not used to people moving around during the service.

"Baby, is it making you horny?"

Gunter sat beside her. He had agreed to come along only after Josie had promised to be in one of his movies. Besides, he was sort of intrigued by the phenomenon of Brother Red Hair. Being a European, this was even more far out for him than it was for Josie. Marcy sat on her other side. He also noticed the bevy of beauties who were scattered throughout the church. They all wore headsets and he figured that they were probably part of Red's organization. The sight of these girls was not lost on Marcy and Josie either.

"Shut up, I'm trying to listen," he said after Marcy winked at him.

They were both wearing dresses. Gunter, however, looked more like he was going to a nightclub than he was a church. He had on a pair of black leather pants and a half open silk shirt.

Josie looked around at the other members of the congregation. It contained people from all walks of life. There were homeless people and streetwalkers as well as people in nice clothes. There were old people, young people, thin people and fat people. You name it, they were there. Josie also took a look around the Cardboard Cathedral. It wasn't really made of cardboard, as she had sort of suspected. It was just the old civic coliseum. It was decorated with purple curtains and a scant few other decorations. Mostly, it was just your typical auditorium. Still, it was filled with something that was absolutely indescribable. It was filled with the force of Red's personality, but more than that, it was filled with love. The place was huge and it was absolutely packed. She was just able to see Sister Gwen and Brother Farlin sitting down on the front row.

As Josie listened to Red's words, she couldn't help but feel something stirring in deep inside her. Her hormones were surging at the sight of Brother Red down there shouting out the message. She just didn't know what was coming over her. Maybe it was the heat. The coliseum was pretty hot and stuffy. Maybe it was the pantyhose. She certainly wasn't used to wearing anything like that. She wasn't even sure why she had worn them. She guessed it was because her mother had always told her to wear pantyhose whenever she went to church. "It's more ladylike," she had said.

Of course, she remembered to wear her black bra and panties. Perhaps that's why she was so constricted. Was a person supposed to wear panties with pantyhose? Since she never wore underwear, it was a little unclear for her. Then again, maybe the cause was something else. It was more like animal magnetism. And she could certainly tell that Brother Red had a lot of that.

"How about now, baby?" Gunter said again. "I know I'm horny."

Marcy crossed and uncrossed her legs and smiled at him. She looked over at Josie who was entranced.

The thing about it was that Josie really was horny. She was really feeling to feel lightheaded. Her breathing was shallow and she felt an odd sort of excitement from the service. She ached to start playing with herself, but didn't because she was in church.

Of course, Brother Red Hair knew for a fact that she was in the audience. It was more than just a gut feeling. His staff had been on the lookout for her. He had to struggle not to get a hard-on when he finally spotted her. He fought the urge to masturbate in front of the congregation. Still, he had to get closer to her. When he saw her, began to play to her. As he did this, he suddenly had an idea.

He stopped preaching for a second and took out his handkerchief and mopped his brow.

"Brothers and Sisters," he began. "I'm really feeling the spirit today. I'm really feeling it take a hold of me. Does that ever happen to you? The spirit just gets a hold of you and makes you just want to run."

He looked feverishly around the congregation and was pleased to see that Josie was transfixed by his service.

Red gave a big smile and suddenly took off running the aisles of the church.

"Whoooo!" He yelled and waved his hands above his hands as he ran.

He ran down one and then the next until finally he was running down the one in which Josie was seated.

Josie's heartbeat quickened as he approached. Her breathing quickened and she could feel herself becoming flushed. Even Gunter and Marcy stopped their flirting as he approached. Her mouth began to water at the sight of his enormous penis which was bouncing within his pants at every step. Her head swam more and more with each approaching step. She was being consumed with horniness and it felt as all the blood was running out of her head. It was just too much to take as she gazed up upon Red's smiling face, growing closer and closer. His cock...

Then suddenly, he was beside Josie.

She looked up at him in awe and when he smiled and put his hand out and touched her on the head, her world suddenly went black.

7

"Brothers and sisters, puhleeze give the young lady some air! Puhleeze, step back and give me some room to work!" Red waved off the crowd as they gathered around Josie's prone body. She had been unconscious for about thirty seconds and Red knew that he was going to have to do something quick.

"Please step back, brothers and sisters, Brother Red is gonna heal this young lady," Brother Abernathy said as he stepped up and started working as crowd control. Brother Myrtlewood picked up the pace on the organ and soon people were running the aisles and rejoicing in time to the music. They clapped their hands like crazy people and if it had been a rock concert instead of a church service, there would have surely been stage diving. Some people even began hopping over the pews. It was an amazing sight. To an outside observer, it would have looked more like an insane asylum than a church.

Marcy was down at Josie's side, fanning her with her hand, trying to get her to wake up.

"Josie, wake up!" She tried to shoo people away. "Please give her some air!"

She turned to Gunter. "Pick her up and let's take her to the hospital!"

Gunter stepped over Josie and bent down to pick her up, but Brother Abernathy gently pushed him aside.

"It'll be okay. Let Brother Red here take a look."

"You're kidding, right?" Gunter sputtered.

Red smiled and knelt over Josie. "No, Brother, he's not kidding. I'm gonna heal this here girl!"

Brother Abernathy looked knowingly at Marcy and Gunter. "He's gonna lay his hands on her."

Red grinned up at them like he was Buddha or something. Being the charismatic individual he was, he had been through this dozens of times. Pretty girls all over the world had swooned over him. Sometimes, they would just get so worked up that they would just faint right there on the spot. This was nothing new and he knew just the trick to revive her.

Red knelt down over her and placed his hands on her stomach. He gently rubbed it and worked his way up to her breasts. He rubbed them slowly, cupping them and really giving them a sensual massage. He noticed with glee that Josie was wearing the black bra. He was certain that she had worn the panties as well. This was almost too much to take. He looked over at Marcy and wondered if she had remembered as well. He gave her a little wink.

Marcy gave a slight smile back and noticed with mixed feelings the enormous bulge growing in Red's trousers.

"What do you think you're doing?" Marcy said, not taking her eyes off the bulge. Was it ever going to stop getting larger, she thought to herself.

"Oh, nobody lays on hands like Brother Red," a toothless old woman exclaimed and went back to dancing and waving her hands in the air and speaking in tongues.

Brother Abernathy also gave her a little smile. Marcy noticed that he had an erection as well. It was nothing to sneeze at either.

Red continued to work on Josie, rubbing her breasts and putting one hand up her skirt. He rubbed her pussy a little harder than he had her breasts, and suddenly she started moving a little bit. She was still unconscious but she was waking up.

Red moved his body so his erection was right in front of her face, and started to really work her pussy. After a few seconds, the still unconscious Julie began to make a sucking motion with her lips. Red moved his penis, which was still in his pants, to her mouth and she began to gently gnaw on it. He suddenly picked up the pace on her pussy and after a few more seconds, she began to buck and soon was flailing and gasping with a gigantic orgasm.

Then, as she came, she came to, still mouthing Red's penis.

Everybody in the congregation began to cheer.

She looked up at Red, who was smiling benevolently down at her. He removed the finger he had had inside her and licked it. Then he smoothed the hair on her head.

Some women would have felt violated after being molested in their sleep like that, but Josie amazingly was not. She looked up at Red and felt a devotion that she had never felt for anyone before in her life. It was like a message had been sent to her and for the first time in her life she truly felt like she had a purpose. She knew what she was meant to do. She knew that she was meant to follow this man.

Brother Abernathy reached down and helped herto stand, being sure to feel her up a little as he steadied her on her feet. "You were out for quite a few minutes, Miss. But thankfully, Brother Red here was able to bring you back."

People patted Red on the back.

"It wasn't me, brothers and sisters. I'm just a tool. I think we know who was responsible." Red tried not to sound too insincere. He wasn't really, but sometimes playing the part of the TV preacher was even a little bit more than even he could bear.

Gunter and Marcy were flabbergasted. Marcy couldn't believe that Red's penis was so large and Gunter couldn't believe what he had just seen Red get away with. Maybe he was in the wrong game, after all. Being in porn meant that you could get laid any time you wanted, but the money wasn't always that great. But from what he could tell about being a preacher, it was about getting laid and making lots of money. His mind was swimming with possibilities.

Josie stared around for a minute at the crowd that had gathered around her. Brother Myrtlewood was wailing on the Hammond and people were dancing in the aisles in joyous celebration of Brother Red's laying on of hands.

She looked at Red who continued to smile at her. "When is your next service? I want to be here."

Marcy looked at his erection. It hadn't shrunk one bit. It strained to be released from his pants and she couldn't help but moisten her lips at the sight of it. Still, she didn't really know about all of this. She had been raised a strict Seventh Day Adventist and had had enough of church when she was a kid. She sure didn't want to get that started again. But then she happened to catch a glimpse of Brother Abernathy. His penis was still hard as well and she could catch the outline of the head through his tight thin pants. She felt her face flush and her pussy get warm. The sight of the two monster cocks was more than enough to convince her.

"Me, too," she said without hesitating.

Gunter looked around at all the gorgeous girls that Red had working for him and realized that there might be something to this religion thing after all. He might learn how to start his own thing.

"I want to join as well."

Red put his arms around them and gave them a big hug.

"Welcome home, brother and sisters. Welcome home."

"Do you think that this dildo is big enough?" Priscilla said as she picked up a black nine-inch jelly dong. She liked the feel of it, but she didn't want to buy just any old thing. She had done that many times in the past and, as a result, had lots of sextoys that she rarely used. Of course, they were always a hit at the swing parties she and Hal hosted, but this time she really wanted something that was going to knock her socks off.

"I don't know, honey. You know how hot you get sometimes," Hal said as he inspected a Swedish cock ring set. He wasn't really that much into cock rings, but what the hell, you only live once, he thought. He also wondered if they were any different from the Dutch cock ring set he had gotten the previous year.

Priscilla and Hal were doing some shopping for Bob and Jenny's anniversary party. They had already bought presents for both Bob and Jenny and were now looking for something for themselves. Priscilla had bought Jenny an elaborate strap-on set and for Bob they had gotten a g-string with an elephant's head as the crotch piece. Naturally, this was a practical joke. They had also bought them a shiatsu massager. Priscilla couldn't wait to try out the strap-on on Jenny and Hal couldn't wait to watch.

"Do you have anything bigger than this?" Priscilla asked the clerk. He was a typically dumpy guy in his twenties with a shaved head and numerous facial piercings.

"The twelve-inchers are on the wall to your left," he said cheerfully.

"Oh, thanks."

As they looked at the brightly colored dildos, Priscilla turned to Hal.

"Do you think we should buy Josie something? After all, she's in the adult biz. She might really appreciate it."

Hal shook his head. "No, I don't think it's a good idea. She might think we're weird or something. You know how these kids are. It's okay if it's their idea, but if Mom and Dad come on board, all of a sudden, it's square."

"Oh, I understand what you're saying, but eventually, we'll have to tell her about us."

Hal sighed. "I know. But let's wait until the right time, okay?"

Priscilla nodded. "Whenever that is," she said under her breath.

Hal heard her, but didn't say anything.

"Oh, here's a nice one," she said and picked up a twelve inch black one.

"That is a good one. It'll fit into your strap-on thing, too."

"Yeah, you're right," she said.

After paying for their purchases, they went home.

"I'm gonna call her, just to see how's she doing," Hal said putting the bags down on the kitchen table. "She may try to call tonight while we're gone."

"Okay. I need to talk to her about what she wants me to do about her car tags, anyway," Priscilla said.

Hal picked up the phone.

"What time is it out there, Hal?"

Hal looked at his watch. "It's around two."

He dialed the number and Josie picked up after one ring.

"Oh, hello, baby. How's it going?" Hal asked.

Priscilla watched with a little interest as Hal listened to what sounded like an enormous amount of chattering coming from the other side of the line. This went on for a few minutes, with Hal interjecting a, "That's nice," or "Good for you," every so often. Eventually, Hal said goodbye absently and hung up the phone.

"Hal! Why did you hang up for? You knew I wanted to talk to her."

"Oh, I'm sorry," he mumbled and stared off into space.

"What's wrong? What did she say?"

Dazed, he looked at her, barely able to speak.

"She's not pregnant is she? Please don't say she's pregnant!" Priscilla was almost frantic.

Hal slowly shook his head.

"No, it's nothing like that. It's worse in a way. I guess you were right. We really should have told her about us. Maybe this wouldn't have happened. She would have known our values and seen that it's okay to be sexual. Maybe they wouldn't have been able to get to her."

Priscilla could already feel her eyes starting to tear up. She didn't know what was going on, but she knew it had to be bad.

"Well, what is it? Tell me! Maybe it's not as bad as you think."

Stonefaced, he stared at her.

"Our daughter's a religious fanatic."

9

Today's the day, Josie thought to herself as she and Marcy got out of the car.

"Don't forget the tracts," Josie said as she checked her makeup in the side mirror.

"I've got them," Marcy said as she smoothed down her skirt and adjusted her top so her cleavage didn't show that much. She was trying to look somewhat respectable for their first day of witnessing. She and Josie were dressed in their Sunday best. They were wearing short black skirts and conservative white tops.

However, Marcy's boobs were just so big that no matter how conservative the top, it was impossible for her to conceal them.

Of course, they had both remembered to wear their black bras and panties. Red wasn't going to be around to see, so they didn't really know why they made this decision. It just seemed like the right thing to do.

"Okay. Let's get started," Josie said breathily as she closed the door to her Nissan.

Never in a million years, would Josie ever have thought that she would be going door to door, handing out tracts and telling people about Brother Red's church. While she had come from a fairly conservative background, she and her family had never done anything like this. They had always just gone to church, listened to the service and then gone home. It was just a routine thing for her as a girl. It was a social event more than anything else. This, however, was something else entirely. After she had been healed by Brother Red, she had felt a devotion and love so great that she just knew that she had to be a part of it. She knew that she had to start contributing. She was actually getting involved.

Marcy, on the other hand, had done this sort of thing a zillion times when she was a child. She had grown up a Seventh Day Adventist and had regularly gone around trying to convert and browbeat others to her way of thinking. As a girl, she had routinely chastised meateaters and Sunday keepers as a part of her religious commitment. Of course, she had never really had any sort of freewill in the matter. It was just something that her parents had made her do. So, it was inevitable that once she left home, she had opened her eyes to the fact that most of the people in the world didn't think like her and, as a result, had fallen out of it. She didn't go to church anymore and while she was still a vegetarian, she did enjoy a good cock whenever she could get one. It was just a miracle that she had found a church with so many big cocked men in leadership positions. This had never been the case with the church she grew up in.

After being healed, Josie, along with Marcy and Gunter, had started going to the Cardboard Cathedral on a regular basis. Gunter wasn't really up with the going door to door stuff, though he promised to go a few times just to figure out how to do it. Josie noted that he seemed to be more interested in taking notes of how the operation ran rather than in experiencing the sheer joy that was the Brother Red Hair religious experience. She had also noted that Marcy couldn't keep her eyes above Brother Red's waistline. She wanted a taste of his cock as well, but at least she wasn't so obvious about it.

When they had first started regularly attending, Josie had felt a little guilty about being a porno actress. She wondered if it was right that she was going to church and still fucking on film. Sister Gwen, though, assuaged her fears.

"Josie, I've told you before. It takes all kinds of people to contribute. I'm sure that Brother Red wouldn't want you to change for anything."

Josie was a little relieved. She didn't know what she was going to do if she had to give up her job. After all, she had a car payment and rent to think about.

Red, of course, had already told Sister Gwen that under no circumstances was she to let Josie stop being a porno actress.

When Josie and Marcy walked about a block up the sidewalk, Josie stopped.

"Well, what about this one?" She pointed to a little A-frame house just to their right.

"I guess it's as good as any," Marcy said and put out her cigarette.

"We can start here and work our way back to the car."

"Okay."

"I'm just so nervous," Josie said as they started walking.

"It's going to be okay. I used to do this kind of thing all the time when I was a kid."

"Oh, yeah, that's right. It's just that I don't want to say the wrong thing or anything," Josie said.

"Well, you remember what Sister Gwen said?"

"Do whatever it takes to get them into church," Josie said.

"Just don't give up too easily," Marcy added. "The biggest thing is getting in the door. That's what they always told us when I was a kid. You can't work on them unless they feel comfortable enough to let you in."

Once at the house, Josie rang the doorbell. No one answered. She rang it again and still no one answered, although they could hear someone, possibly a group of people rustling around.

"Ring it one more time," Marcy said. "If they don't answer, we'll just leave a tract and go to the next house."

Josie nodded. But just as she reached out to ring the doorbell again, the door flew open. Josie and Marcy jumped back in shock.

"What do you want?" A big, muscle-bound, tattooed biker-type looked wildly out the door. "You ain't the cops, are you? You've got to tell me if you are."

"No…, we're not the cops, we're just spreading the good news," Josie said and tried to smile.

"What do they want?" Another biker type, even bigger than the other one, walked up behind the other type.

"They say they're here to tell us the good news," the first one said.

"Yes," Marcy said, quickly checking out their packages through their dirty, tight jeans. She definitely liked what she saw. "We're here to tell you about Brother Red Hair and *The Church of What's Happenin' Now*. If you just have a minute…"

Suddenly the first biker started grinning and checking her out. "Well, why didn't you ladies say that in the first place."

He opened the door and gestured for them to come in. The second biker type smiled his best smile as well. "Come on in."

Josie looked at Marcy as if to say, do you think we should be doing this?

"Remember what Sister Gwen said. Whatever it takes," Marcy said.

"Yes," Josie repeated. "Whatever it takes."

The two girls walked in and were immediately confronted by the overwhelming smells of sweat, grease, stale beer and marijuana.

"Now, have a seat, girls, and tell us what you want."

Josie and Marcy hesitantly sat down in a broken down loveseat. They could see that in addition to the two bikers who greeted them at the door, there were three more in there as well. They were just as big as the other two. A porno movie played on a brand new big screen TV which was probably stolen.

Marcy nudged Josie. The girl getting fucked on screen was a friend of theirs.

Josie cleared her throat. "What would you do if I said that I could tell you something that would change your life?"

"I would say, let's hear it," the first biker said.

"Okay…" Josie started.

"Hey, hold on a second," the second biker said. "I'm not sure if we're gonna be able to concentrate on what you're saying or not."

"What do you mean?" Marcy said.

"Well, me and the boys were kind of in the middle of watching this here porno movie and I don't know if we're gonna be able to hear about your church. We've got our minds on other things, if you know what I mean." He couldn't help but start grinning.

Josie looked around and saw that all the bikers were nursing enormous hard-ons. She could feel herself getting wet at the very thought of taking on all these guys. She glanced at Marcy, who was already salivating, and could tell that she was thinking the same thing.

"Now, if you girls want to take care of us first, we'll be able to listen to you with a clear head…"

Marcy nudged Josie. "Whatever it takes."

Josie was on her knees and had the second biker's cock out of his pants before he was able to finish talking. Marcy had her skirt off and was over at the three other bikers almost as quick. All the bikers gathered around her as she got down on her knees and started sucking their fully engorged cocks. They were all monster-sized, Marcy thought as she attempted to deepthroat the first one. She couldn't wait for them to start fucking her. Meanwhile, Josie had her hands full with the first and second biker. Her head bobbed up and down, going from cock to cock. To be so greasy and dirty looking, the biker's penises were surprisingly clean. She figured that these particular bikers were more posers than anything else, probably. The bikers looked at each other and couldn't help but smile at their good fortune. Josie was able to bring the pre-cum up fast. She had to slow down or these guys were going to shoot too fast. She couldn't let this day go without being fucked three ways to Sunday by these big dicks.

Slowing the pace down just a bit, so they wouldn't come too quickly, she stood and led the two bikers by the dicks over to where Marcy was servicing the other three. From there she and Marcy swapped places and she was able to get a taste of the other three. After having every dick in her mouth at least twice, the two girls turned up the pace a little bit. They pulled off the rest of their clothes.

"Now, you guys are gonna fuck the living shit out of us. Do you think you can handle that?" Josie said as she rubbed her ass against the first biker.

"I don't think that's gonna be a problem," he said.

Josie grabbed his dick and pulled him down to the floor and guided him into her doggy style. She bucked against him hard and came within seconds. She reached out and grabbed one of the other bikers and sucked him as hard as she could. She could see his eyes rolling back in his head with ecstasy. Marcy, on the other hand was going for the double penetration with two of other bikers while she sucked the other one off. Marcy wailed as she came repeatedly at the double fucking.

"I'm gonna blow!" The second biker said as he pounded into Josie.

"Well, switch with this guy. I don't want to waste any of your cum," Josie said breathlessly. At that, the two bikers switched and she started sucking the second biker while the other aggressively started fucking her, bringing her to another orgasm.

"Oh my God!" the second biker said as Josie began sucking the cum out of his dick. She was like a vacuum cleaner. He came what seemed like a quart and she just kept sucking and swallowing. Pretty soon, the other guy was ready to cum and Josie took care of him in the same way. Then she made her way over to Marcy who was in the process of getting her first load of the day. The biker stood and pumped it into her mouth and as soon as he was finished, Josie went over and french kissed her, taking the snowball into her mouth and swallowing every bit.

She then masturbated as she watched the other two bikers pull out of Marcy and cum simultaneously onto her face. Josie went over to help her clean up, licking and wiping off the cum with her fingers. Josie came again as she swallowed the last bit of jizz.

After they had finished fucking and everyone had their clothes on, Josie and Marcy sat down and told the bikers all about Brother Red's ministry. The bikers listened with rapt attention.

"So, what do you think, fellas? Don't you want to contribute to something good?" Marcy said as she smoothed her skirt and finished the initial presentation.

"Yeah, if you would just go and listen for yourself to what Brother Red has to say, you'll see what we're talking about," Josie said, still savoring the taste of cum in her mouth.

"Do you think you can do us all again?" the second biker said as he started rubbing his penis. "We'll definitely go to church if you do us again."

Josie looked at Marcy. "Well, I am still kind of horny."

"And you remember what Sister Gwen said," Marcy added.

"Whatever it takes," Josie added.

With that, both girls got down on their knees and got to work. Again.

10

Of course, Red was elated after Sister Gwen told him that Josie was already going out and doing the church's work. He had been sure that she would eventually start volunteering, but so soon? Just how good was that? He was positive that it would be no time at all before she was a full-fledged member of his staff. Just like Sister Gwen and all the other girls before her. He wasn't that concerned about Marcy. He knew from the way she stared at his cock that she wasn't leaving. It was a definitely a good day at the Cardboard Cathedral. Red felt he was going to burst with joy after he heard the news.

"Thank you for the good news, Sister Gwen! Such wonderful news has never come from your mouth."

He gazed at Sister Gwen who looked back at him with a look of sheer joy. She was unable to speak at the time, however, because she had Brother Abernathy's rock hard, big black cock in her mouth. Red was on the vaginal side of a double penetration with Brother Myrtlewood pounding her in her ass. Brother Farlin was taking pictures and jerking off. Sister Gwen convulsed occasionally as she came and took a break from Brother Abernathy's cock to squeal with delight. Dutifully she always went back to sucking. After a bit of this, they switched around, playing musical chairs with her orifices. Red had found that gangbanging Sister Gwen was always good for the morale of the staff. She certainly enjoyed it.

After she came for the umpteenth time, the men were finally ready for some relief. Fucking Sister Gwen was hard but satisfying work and they all deserved a reward. She got down on her knees and gathered all them around her and drained them all. After they had shot their loads into her mouth and she was able to swallow every drop was she able to speak.

"Don't worry, Brother Red," she said as she licked the cum off her lips. "I'll make sure she doesn't quit or get discouraged. And she'll always wear black underwear." She then grabbed Red's penis and sucked him a little more, just to make sure that she had gotten it all.

"Oh, yes!" Red moaned, thinking about Josie in a black bra.

She then did the same with Brother Abernathy and Brother Myrtlewood.

"Oh, yeah, Sister. Oh, yeah," Brother Abernathy moaned as she sucked the remaining drops of cum from his big black penis. She even took Brother Farlin's load, just so he didn't feel left out.

"You did get some good pictures of her deepthroating Brother Abernathy, didn't you?" Brother Myrtlewood said as Brother Farlin pulled his dick from Sister Gwen's mouth.

"Oh, yeah, I always do."

The purpose of the pictures was to give them something happy to look at whenever life's problems started getting them down. Red was a strong believer in thinking happy thoughts and what best brought about happy thoughts? Happy pictures of course! Of course, he fully trusted that Brother Farlin wouldn't do anything crazy with the pictures like send them to the newspaper or anything.

After they were finished, Brother Abernathy took a small bag of marijuana from his suit pocket and rolled up a joint. He was an expert when it came to marijuana and rolling a joint was his forte. Even with his eyes shut, he could roll one that looked just like a store bought cigarette. He lit it and passed it around. Red took a hit and uncapped the bottle of Canadian Club that he had stashed in his top desk drawer. When it was Myrtlewood's turn with the joint, he was a little slow to pass it back.

"Yo, man, pass that hogleg down to the little lady," Brother Abernathy said.

"Oh, sorry," Brother Myrtlewood said sheepishly and passed it on to Sister Gwen.

"Isn't that the most glorious news you've heard today, brothers?" Red said again, for about the fifteenth time that that evening.

"Red," Brother Abernathy said as he took a hit off the joint. "Just what exactly is so important about this particular girl? I mean, I know it's important to get new members into the church and to get people on the right path, but why the emphasis on her? I mean, if it's a ho you want, they're a dime a dozen."

Red looked at him with a big smile. "I don't want her to be my ho, Brother Abernathy. I want her to be my girlfriend!"

All the people in the room looked at him like he was a little bit crazy at this exclamation. Brother Myrtlewood did a spittake with the Canadian Club.

"Not meaning any disrespect or anything, but don't you think you're kinda going about it in a kind of roundabout way, Red?"

"Yeah, that's what I was thinking," Brother Abernathy said.

Red shook his head and smiled.

Sister Gwen could see through him and was touched.

"Don't you guys see? He wants to impress her. He's just being old-fashioned. I think it's so sweet." She pinched Red on the cheek and he couldn't help but blush.

"She's just so pretty! I just can't for the opportunity to ask her out!"

Brother Abernathy looked at Red a little dubiously. "But don't you think that she might have a problem with all of this?"

"Oh, I don't think so, brother." Red smiled.

"She's a regular little slut," Sister Gwen said matter of factly. "She makes porno films. Nasty ones."

"And that's why I'm so in love with her!" Red beamed.

"She's just so sexy, I just want to eat her up!" Sister Gwen said before she thought about it. Red smiled.

They sat around smoking pot and drinking for about thirty more minutes. Eventually, Brother Abernathy and Brother Myrtlewood began to get a little restless.

"Yo, Red, what time is it?"

Red looked at his Rolex. "It's around midnight."

"Well, I don't know about everybody else, but I think we need to go out and witness to some new females."

"Sounds like a good idea to me," Brother Myrtlewood said. "What about you Farlin?"

"I'm ready."

"How about you Gwen? You want to go pick up some chicks and convert them?"

"Convert them to what?" She purred. "Of course, I'm up for it."

"Red?"

Red smiled at all of them and gently nodded his head. "Do you even have to ask?"

They quickly put on their clothes and headed out to do a little witnessing.

"Strip clubs here we come!" Brother Myrtlewood whooped as they got into Red's Cadillac.

"Don't forget about the massage parlor!" Brother Farlin said, but not before closing his thumb in the door. He hollered as he jerked the thumb back. It didn't look too bad, but he was probably going to lose the thumbnail. He tried his best not to start whining in pain.

"Think you can heal that?" Brother Abernathy said to Red as he examined Brother Farlin's thumb.

They all burst out laughing. Even Brother Farlin.

11

The next week went by like a whirlwind for Josie. She was just brimming over with enthusiasm. She had never been so excited about anything in her life. Not even sex and that was saying something. The odd thing about it was that the zeal she felt for *What's Happenin' Now* and Brother Red Hair carried over to her career too. She was just so much more into her performances than she had ever been before. Having a purpose just made her horny, she supposed. Regardless, she was insatiable on the set. The guys and girls down at *Solid Gold Medallion,* the company she mainly shot for, couldn't help but comment on it.

"All right, let's have the money shot!" The director barked.

At the moment a stud named Johnny Stiffcock pulled out of Josie's pussy and she got down on her knees and prepared to accept his load. He was big, but she was able to deepthroat him a couple of times before he shot it. He came a lot and she eagerly started deepthroating him again after the camera had captured the initial money shot. She loved it when a guy shot straight into her throat. It was kind of like eating an oyster, she thought. The movie was titled, appropriately enough, *All the Ladies Love Johnny Stiffcock*.

"Damn, girl, what's going on with you? I knew you could suck dick, but damn!" Johnny said breathlessly after the director stopped filming. He couldn't get over how she had just worn him out. She had literally drained him of all his cum and energy. He was exhausted.

Josie licked her lips.

"It's amazing what you can do when you finally figure out what you're put on this earth for." She smiled broadly.

"Well, I definitely know one thing you're good for," the director laughed as he gave her a quick feel. Johnny couldn't help but slap her ass as he moved away.

Solid Gold Medallion was the biggest porn outfits on the west coast, and it was Josie's dream to be one of their contract girls. She was currently a free lancer, shooting for whomever her agent sent her to. Marcy was already a contract girl there and had been trying to get them to pick Josie up for a good while. She knew that Josie would eventually be a contract girl somewhere. She was just too beautiful and sexy not to be. She just hoped that it would be at *Solid Gold*.

Marcy wandered over to Josie from the kitchen. The scene had been shot in the living room of the house. She was still nude from her scene about an hour earlier. She gave Josie a hug and continued to stay close and gently stroked her ass as they talked.

"Do you think they're ready for the tracts?" Josie said excitedly and reciprocated by nuzzling Marcy's big breasts. Those breasts were Josie's biggest weakness, maybe even more so than cock. She didn't know why , but she couldn't fathom what it would be like not to be able to touch or kiss them.

"I don't know. I guess we could find out," she began to stroke Josie's pussy as they talked.

"So, what are you girls talking about?" A sexy English voice purred right behind Josie.

It was Vanessa Perkins, a hot new starlet from Britain. She was a sexy and nasty brunette. She was going to be huge.

"Oh, we're talking about our church activities," Josie said breathlessly as Vanessa began to nuzzle her neck and rub her pussy from behind.

The girls were too wrapped up to see that the crew and other actors had all gathered around them and were watching the show. The director silently motioned the cameraman to turn on the camera. He surreptitiously began to film them.

"Sounds brilliant," Vanessa said and got down on her knees and began eating Josie out from behind.

Marcy dropped down to her knees and started eating Josie out from the front as well.

"Oh, it is," she said and kissed Vanessa as both girls began to feast on Josie's pussy.

It didn't take Josie long to be overcome by the two girls eating her pussy. She came soon thereafter. After she came, Vanessa and Marcy began fingering themselves. They soon pulled Josie down on the floor and they quickly formed a daisy chain. Marcy licked Josie and Josie licked Vanessa. The room was soon filled by the sounds of the girls moaning in orgasm. The girls were so wet that when Vanessa and Josie began scissoring each other's pussies, they couldn't help but make a smacking sound. Marcy hunched the side of Vanessa's thigh as they all bucked themselves into a full tilt frenzy.

After the girls had all orgasmed, the cast and crew burst into applause. The girls started and finally took a look around them. They started laughing when they saw their audience.

The director walked over to them. "All I've got to say, girls, is that I'm glad we had the camera up."

"You mean you filmed it?" Josie asked.

"Damn straight I did. And don't worry, you'll get paid. You don't get any girl/girl/girl scenes better than that. It was just so intense that I almost jizzed my pants just sitting here."

Josie thought for a second and then whispered something to Marcy, who smiled and nodded her head.

"Instead of paying us with money, there's something else I would like you to do for us."

"Sure, girls, you name it."

Josie smiled.

"Great! This will only take about thirty minutes. Marcy, let's go get the tract literature."

The director looked at Vanessa. She shrugged her shoulders. She didn't have a clue as to what was going on, but she was about to find out.

12

The morning sun was so bright that Red almost had to put on his sunglasses just to think. Maybe it was because he was a little hungover. He didn't know what it was, but sitting at the patio of the restaurant, everything was bright.

Red put out his cigarette and looked around at the people at his table. If he looked over his plate of eggs and pancakes he could see Brother Abernathy chowing down on a plate full of bacon and eggs. If he looked over his coffee he could see Sister Gwen eating a grapefruit. If he looked under the table, he could not only see up her skirt, he could also see her fingering the blonde stripper sitting next to her. If he continued to look under the table, he could see the stripper giving Brother Myrtlewood a handjob, who was, in turn, fingering another stripper, a brunette. And that brought them full circle around to him. But no, there was someone else, someone sitting right beside him. It was Brother Farlin. He was just sitting there eating oatmeal and staring into space. He was also jerking off.

He looked at all their clothes. They were all rumpled and looked as though they had been slept in, even though there hadn't been any sleeping. Red sighed with satisfaction. This was such a great life. He was so glad that he had started his church. He couldn't imagine life any other way. No, wait, there was another way. He could imagine it with Josie by his side. Aside from healing the girl, he didn't know her. However, he had seen enough of her movies to know that he would like her. And he had had the dream. He got hard instantly when he thought about her sitting in his congregation with her black bra and panties.

After they had left the office the night before, they had first tried their luck picking up prostitutes. They managed to get two black girls in the car but were unable to witness to them. After pulling the Cadillac into the parking lot of an electronics store, all the girls wanted to do was suck them all off. They even ate Sister Gwen out.

"I've already got a church," one of them said. "I don't need another one."

"But, baby, this is a different kind of church," Brother Abernathy said breathily as the other one took his massive dick deep in her throat.

"Shut up, moonie and just get yo nut off. I don't want to hear no more." Then she started sucking Brother Myrtlewood. She was like a vacuum cleaner because she had him cumming in a matter of seconds.

The other girl, while enthusiastic, seemed to have a little trouble keeping Brother Abernathy's cock deepthroated for any length of time. Sister Gwen got down there with her and gave her a few pointers.

"Just relax your throat," she said as she took the big black cock in her hands. It was so big that both of her hands didn't even come close to covering it. "Just like this." With that, she took the cock completely down her throat. She had so much of it in her throat that her lips were touching Brother Abernathy's nuts.

"Damn, girl!" the prostitute said. "I can't believe you just deepthroated that big ol'dick. You really know what you're doing."

"I used to be a whore just like you. Until I met Brother Red."

The prostitute looked at her incredulously. Sister Gwen leaned in close to her.

"Brother Red's cock is even bigger than this one," she whispered.

The prostitute looked at Red and couldn't help but smack her lips.

Sister Gwen offered her a tract and the girl took it and put it in her purse. She did it quickly before the other girl, the one who already had a church, could see her.

After taking all of Brother Abernathy's creamy load, she then went to the front seat and started on Red. He was already as hard as a rock.

"Damn, that girl was right about you. I ain't seen too many white boys with a dick this big."

"I'll admit that I've been blessed," Red smiled.

The prostitute went to work and sucked him hard. Using Sister Gwen's technique, she was able to completely deepthroat him up to his balls. Up and down, up and down, she went. She started fingering herself because it was making her so hot. It was obvious that she was wanting it, so when she started tasting precum, she couldn't take any more.

"I'm sorry, but I've just got to get on top of that thang."

"Be my guest, sister."

The prostitute was on top of him in seconds flat. Immediately she started bucking him like she was going crazy. She ground down on him and Red loved every second of it. This girl really knew how to fuck and she was giving him the deluxe treatment. His big cock slid in and out, and she shuddered with orgasms.

"Oh, shit! Damn! Shit! Fuck me, you motherfucker!" she yelled during each one. But Red just kept on fucking.

In the back seat, Sister Gwen was being eaten out and watching the action up in the front seat and was cumming so hard that she couldn't see straight. Brother Farlin watched, jerking off, waiting his turn.

"You better cum in my pussy, you motherfucker!" Red's prostitute said.

"If that's what you want."

With that, Red started pumping his spunk into her. He sucked on her big brown titties as he came. When he was finished, the girl got off him and cleaned off his dick with her mouth.

"That was so good, I think I may have to give you a discount."

Red laughed.

"Get that pussy back here!" Sister Gwen hollered as she came. The girl had been munching on her pussy like it was Big Mac extra value meal.

The prostitute went to the back seat and climbed up on Sister Gwen's face. Sister Gwen eagerly ate out all Red's cum from her pussy. And then came again.

"Damn, that's some kinky shit!" The prostitute who had been eating Sister Gwen said as she watched Sister Gwen licking her lips.

After that, the two prostitutes then went to work on Brother Farlin. Within seconds, he blasted his cum over both the girls' faces. This was after they had instructed him to cum in their mouths.

They looked a little pissed off at first, but when Sister Gwen offered to clean it off for them, they calmed down a little.

After that Red tried to witness again, but the girls wouldn't hear any of it.

"Well, pay them out of petty cash then, Brother Farlin."

The girls paid, Brother Red and company went on their way.

Next, they took Red's Cadillac on over to the Va-Va-Voom Room. It was a fairly high-class strip club and they were known there. The girls at the club loved Sister Gwen. They always gave her kisses and free lap-dances. Red knew that they would be able to get at least a couple of girls to come to church with them. Several of girls who worked there were already members. They were always more than happy to see Red and his crew.

Several lapdances and trips to the back room later, here they were at the restaurant eating breakfast. The girls were coming over to the office to see what they could do for the church.

And what the church could do for them.

Looking at the two hot girls made Red salivate. The blonde had a body that would stop a clock and the brunette's tits made him ache with horniness. Yes, these girls were going to definitely be favored members of his church. But his mind kept going back to one thing. No matter how much he wanted to get his hands on them, he still wanted to get with Josie even more.

13

"No, baby, I can't drive you and Marcy to the mall," Gunter said very irritably. "I know you want me to join you in handing out the tracts, but I'm sorry I can't go." Then he added as an afterthought, "Besides, if you wanted me to hand out the tracts, why didn't you just say so?"

He paused for a second. "Goodbye. Yes, baby, I will go to the church with you on Sunday."

Gunter sighed. He was a little annoyed that Josie was trying to trick him into handing out Brother Red Hair's tracts, but that wasn't the reason he didn't want to help. No, the reason he wasn't going to drive them wasn't because he didn't want to, but because he couldn't.

"That damn, piece of scheiss Audi!" He bellowed as he looked out his window. Sure, it was a beautiful car and sure it was from the Fatherland, but what good was it him if it was always breaking down? No, that still wasn't the problem. What he meant to think was what good was the car to him if it was always tearing up and *he couldn't afford to fix it*?

To most people in the porn world, Gunter appeared to be one well-to-do guy. However, what most people didn't realize was that he was always broke. He was a big star in Europe, he was a big star over here and he wore the nicest clothes and jewelry. Plus, he had that beautiful Audi. All this was true, sure, but the problem was that he spent his money just as fast as he made it. It was like he was a middle man for his money. He was just a conveyance between his employers and his creditors. And yes, while it was great to be recognized on the street, an amazing feat for a porno actor, this sort of thing didn't pay to get the car fixed.

Gunter looked at the two girls stoned and asleep on his couch. It was the same two as before and they were still there. They fucked him for their room and board and what he called their "spiritual instruction." For a second, he thought about going through their purses to get some money. Then he realized that they probably didn't have any. The problem was that all he needed was some sort of sensor for the car. It probably wouldn't have even cost that much to fix. If he had actually had some money, that is.

He put on his shoes and sauntered on out of the house and down to the corner supermarket. He was all out of baby oil and whipped cream. He hoped he had enough money for those two items. His credit card was maxed out and he was overdrawn at the bank. It would certainly be embarrassing to have to put back two items. Still, it would be good for him to do something to get his mind off that fucking car. He had to come up with a plan. He had a job the next day, but what good was that going to do him now?

When he got to the supermarket, he started to feel a lot calmer. As he picked up his items, he was certain everything was going to work out. Why was he panicking? As he walked through the store, he contemplated buying some beer, but then remembered that he didn't have any money. Then he started panicking again.

"Damn, German piece of shit!" He said aloud.

"You talking to yourself, buddy?"

"Why you..." Gunter said and looked around. He was standing next to the magazine rack. Standing there looking at a porno magazine and rubbing himself through his pants, was a familiar looking old guy.

"Do I know you?" Gunter said, no longer pissed off. His mind was taken off the fact that the old guy had smarted off to him by the fact that he was trying to remember who he was.

"I don't know. Do I?" The old man continued to rub himself.

Then it hit Gunter. "I know you, you're from the church. You're Brother..."

"Farlin," the old man said. It was Brother Farlin.

Gunter sidled on over to him like he was his best friend or something. He was still trying to get a handle on the church thing.

"So, tell me, baby, what are you doing here? Shouldn't you be at church doing something for Brother Red?"

Brother Farlin rolled his eyes. "Fuck Brother Red. All he wants me to do is take the pictures."

Gunter looked at him curiously. "Pictures?"

"Yeah, I don't always get to join in whenever we gangbang the new girls. Sometimes I can't get my viagra to kick in at the right time. I can't get a hard-on when I need to, and by the time it finally gets up, they're all finished. It sucks."

Gunter looked down at Brother Farlin. His dick was making a tent in his pants.

"Yep, the gangbang was over an hour ago."

"That's terrible," Gunter said. His mind was still turning over the statement about the pictures. "So, he makes you take the pictures of the gangbangs, ja?"

"Hell, I take pictures of everything."

Gunter was still puzzled.

"But isn't he afraid that someone may see these pictures?"

Brother Farlin looked at him dubiously. "How would anybody see them. I've got them all stored on my computer at home."

Gunter couldn't think of a thing to say. The cash registers going off in his head were too distracting.

14

Sunday morning finally came and Josie was all a flutter. She was so excited about going to the Cardboard Cathedral that she was on the verge of pissing her pants. She danced around while she got ready and modeled about three dresses before she finally decided on a sheer white one. She decided that she liked it best because her black bra and panties could be easily seen through it. Marcy had considerably less trouble. She wore a short black skirt, six inch heels and a white top. She figured that Brother Red would be able to see her black bra through the shirt and his imagination could do the rest.

"Gosh, I'm so excited, Marcy!" Josie said as she brushed her hair for the fifth time. "I don't know what it is, but since I've been going to the Cardboard Cathedral, I'm a new person. You would think I wouldn't still be this excited about going, but it seems I'm more excited than the last time I went!"

Marcy nodded. "I know. I can't wait to go either. While I love the sermons, the sight of Brother Red's big dick outlined in those tight pants, just makes the message that much better."

"Oh, I know! And Sister Gwen is so hot!"

"And what about Brother Abernathy! I bet he could throw down on a girl!"

"Yeah, and that Brother Myrtlewood has to be a real freak!" Josie squealed.

"I bet that Brother Farlin is a perv, too." Marcy laughed and put on the rest of her makeup.

Josie sat on the bed and sighed. "I just can't believe that we found such an amazing church. I had almost given up on religion."

After the two girls were ready, they left for church in Marcy's Toyota.

"Don't forget Gunter," Josie said.

"Yeah, his Audi is fucked up again."

"I don't know why he just doesn't buy another one," Josie said and lit up a cigarette. "You know he makes a lot of money."

"I know that he sure knows how to spend it."

They stopped by Gunter's house and honked the horn. Gunter came out about five minutes later, wearing a loose fitting white shirt, tight black jeans and cowboy boots. Again, it looked like he was going to some euro-trash disco. It was obvious that he was from another country.

"Nice outfit," Marcy said sarcastically.

"Thanks, baby. It's my shamen outfit. I think I can focus on the sermon a bit better in it."

Marcy and Josie rolled their eyes.

"Don't you babies think it's cool?" Gunter said as he got into the car.

The girls mumbled something that Gunter took as an affirmative.

After arriving at the church and settling into their seats, Josie took a look around them. Seated all over the church were people from the porn set. Right across the aisle from them she saw Vanessa Perkins and Carmen. She waved at them and they waved back.

"Hey, babies!" Gunter yelled.

Up above them she saw Cedric and just over from him was Jerome. She also saw the director sitting with one of the new starlets.

"I don't know that fucking guy is doing here," Gunter grumbled. "Surely, he isn't thinking that he can start being in the same place as me."

"C'mon, Gunter this is church. What do you have against the director?" Marcy said.

"I don't know. I just don't think he likes the way I fuck. He's an asshole."

Marcy punched him.

Josie took another look around. "Look, Marcy! They're all here! They all listened to us!"

Marcy took a look around and was flabbergasted. She couldn't believe it. They must have made a real impression to get so many people to attend.

Then Josie heard a voice yelling at her from way over on the other side of the building.

"Hey, Josie!"

She looked over and was amazed to see the whole biker gang sitting together. They were wearing clean clothes and everything. Well, they weren't quite clean clothes, but they were cleaner than the ones they had been wearing when the two girls had stopped at their house.

She nudged Marcy and both girls waved at them.

"Well, after a fucking like we gave them, wouldn't you at least be curious about it?" Marcy said matter of factly.

At that time, Brother Myrtlewood started in on the organ like a wildman, making the Hammond jump like a scalded dog. The drummer joined in and pretty soon, people were up and dancing in the aisles and shouting hallelujah. And the service hadn't even started yet. After a few minutes Brother Red ran out and Josie couldn't help but lose her breath for an instant. After he finished smiling and waving at the crowd, Brother Myrtlewood stopped playing. He would only start up again to punctuate Brother Red's comments.

"Brothers and Sisters, I see we've got a lot of new people out there in the congregation today! And to you I just want to say, Welcome! Welcome! Welcome!"

Everybody cheered and erupted into choruses of *Amen!* and *Hallalujah, Brother Red!* Brother Myrtlewood joined in with some crazy organ playing.

Red's eye was immediately drawn to Josie, sitting up in the second tier of the auditorium. He could see her outfit and the black bra and panties through her dress. He got a hard-on instantly. It was obvious through his tight pants. Nothing was left to the imagination. Josie in turn, noticed his hard-on and began to feel her pussy get a little wet. Marcy's mouth began to water. Josie looked over at Vanessa and Carmen and was pleased to see that they both had their skirts up and were very discreetly playing with themselves. She knew that those girls were going to be converted.

After Red got to cranking on the service, it was no holds barred fire and brimstone. He raced through the congregation screaming and shouting. He leaped over the front pews and danced around on the altar. He was like a wild man.

Josie was so stirred by what she saw that she soon found herself screaming *Amen.* It felt good to join in and suddenly she got a strange feeling and she felt the need to get out of her seat. Marcy looked at her like she was crazy, but she just looked around all wild-eyed. The next thing she knew she was dancing in the aisle and before long she was running the aisles just like everyone else. She felt like she was home.

Marcy, however, wasn't quite so moved. She was focused on trying to maneuver herself so she could get a better look at Brother Red's cock. Frankly, she was a little amazed at how much Josie was getting into the service, but it was none of her business as far as she was concerned. Gunter, on the other hand, was just taking it all in and continuing to think over what he had talked about with Brother Farlin. He was tempted to wave at Brother Farlin who was sitting glumly down on the front row, but thought that it would probably just look weird.

The service was great and when all the singing and shouting was over, Josie, Gunter and Marcy got out of the seats and went over to Carmen and Vanessa.

"So, what did you think?" Josie asked excitedly.

"I think he has got the sweetest looking dick I have ever seen," Vanessa said.

"I was just oozing thinking about what he could do with that big thing."

Gunter looked at the girls dubiously. "Why are you girls so interested in his dick when you can have mine anytime you want it?"

"Gunter, I *work* with you, I would be fucking him," Vanessa said. "That man's penis is to die for."

"Yeah, they pay us to fuck you. We'd be fucking him for free." Marcy laughed.

"You babies really know how to make a guy feel good about himself," Gunter said sullenly.

"That's great!" Josie said, not paying attention and trying to get the conversation back on topic. "So, do you think you'll be back?"

Carmen and Vanessa looked at her like she was crazy.

"Are you crazy? It's an honor just to be in the same room as a cock like that. Yes, we'll be back, right Carmen?"

Carmen licked her lips. "I can't wait to meet that man."

Josie laughed. "I can't either."

"I think you girls know that I want to do more than meet him." Marcy laughed.

Just then, Sister Gwen came up.

"Sister Gwen!" Josie said excitedly and gave her a big hug. "Vanessa and Carmen, this is Sister Gwen, she was the one who told me about this place."

Sister Gwen put out her hands to the girls.

"You girls work with Josie and Marcy...and this guy?" She winked at Gunter, who winked back in his most suave manner.

"Yep, we're porn sluts, too," Vanessa said.

"Ooh, I love a British accent," Sister Gwen said and licked her lips.

Vanessa was a little taken aback. She had never been come on to by a woman in a church before.

Sister Gwen turned her attention to Josie.

"Josie, Brother Red noticed all the new faces in the crowd today and knows that you're the one who brought them in."

"But how does he know it was me?"

"He had Brother Farlin ask some of them."

"I was just doing what I thought was right. Spreading the good news, you know?" Josie laughed.

"Yes, we know. Well, anyway, Brother Red was so excited about it that he wanted to meet you."

"Well, he has met me. You know when he healed me?" Josie said.

"He knows this. But he wants to actually get to talk to you. He wants to find out more about you. He wants you to come to his office this afternoon."

Josie was flabbergasted. "He wants...me? To come to his office?"

Sister Gwen smiled. "Yes. He wants to personally express his gratitude for your work."

"He probably just wants to fuck you," Gunter said matter of factly.

Everybody ignored him.

"That's great. I'll be there." Josie was so excited that she couldn't think straight. Brother Red was the most positive influence in her life and here she was going to his office. Then she remembered the outline of his penis in his pants. She couldn't help but moisten her lips.

"I helped too. Do I get to meet him?" Marcy asked.

Sister Gwen smiled mischievously. "Brother Red is going to meet with you later. Right now, he wants you to get know Brother Abernathy and Brother Myrtlewood a little better."

Marcy was wet instantly.

"So, if we help, can we meet him, too?" Carmen said, fidgeting a little. Her pussy was so wet at the thought of Josie fucking Brother Red that she just couldn't stand still.

"Of course. Brother Red always has time to meet sincere young ladies such as yourself."

"Well, count us in," Vanessa said. "Whatever it takes, we'll do it."

"Okay," Sister Gwen smiled. "First of all, you can come back to my office and I'll get you set up." She winked at the two girls then she turned to Josie. "Be there at one o'clock. He's dying to meet you."

Josie gulped and nodded. She couldn't wait.

"But what about me? Don't I get to go back to your office too?" Gunter said as everybody was walking off.

"I guess you're on your own, this time, Fritz," Sister Gwen said.

Gunter grumbled a little bit under his breath as everybody walked off, but then he saw Brother Farlin. Maybe he wasn't going to be on his own, after all.

15

"Good Lord! There she is! On TV!" Hal said as he excitedly jumped up and ran over to the television. He had been in the process of getting a blowjob from Jenny while sitting in a recliner over at Bob and Jenny's place. They lived in a split level in the adjoining subdivision. It was decorated in a very unironic seventies style on the inside, with lots of heavy wood and a neo-medieval feel.

Jenny, needless to say, was a little confused. She had been about to finger herself to orgasm when Hal had jumped up from his blowjob.

"Who?"

Priscilla looked up from looked up from the floor. She was in the process of getting it doggie style from Bob.

"It's Josie! She's running the aisles! At that church!"

Bob just kept pumping, sliding his penis in and out of Priscilla's engorged vagina. The two of them didn't miss a beat as Priscilla turned her attention to the screen.

"I can't believe it! It's even worse than a cult! She's following a fundamentalist!"

"C'mon, Hal," Jenny said as she walked over to him. She got down on her knees and returned to sucking on his still hard penis. "Surely, it's not as bad as you think," she said as she took a breath.

"Oh, it is. She just wasn't raised this way," Hal said as he rubbed Jenny's head and pushed her mouth down further onto his dick. "She was raised an Episcopalian, wasn't she, hon?" He looked at the TV again and saw Red up there on stage, jumping around and clapping his hands. "And just who the hell is that red-headed bastard?" Furious, he quickly grabbed the remote control and turned the television off.

Priscilla's eyes were rolling back in her head at the pounding she was receiving from Bob.

"She's gonna be completely screwed up now," she groaned and rubbed her clit. "Fuck me harder, Bob!"

Bob picked up the pace and slapped her on the ass.

Jenny turned away from Hal's dick and was now presenting her pussy to him. He stuck one finger in her asshole and then stuck his dick in her pussy all the way up to his balls.

"Oh, God, yes!" Jenny shrieked as Hal began to piston her.

Even as he fucked, Hal still couldn't get the sound of the crazy organ music out of his head. As irritated as he was, it was just almost too much for him to handle. Luckily for him though, Jenny was just so damned hot that nothing could deter him from fucking her.

Priscilla was clawing the carpet as Bob pumped her hard. She hadn't been fucked like this since the last time he had fucked her. Bob was no spring chicken, but he fucked better than most guys half his age. He was a little over forty, so the math was pretty easy. She marked it up to experience. He was almost as good as the black kid down at the paint store. She had repainted the entire house twice because of him. She just couldn't get enough of his jizz. She had even considered freezing some of it, to have whenever she started feeling horny, but she realized that people might think she was a little crazy and decided not to do it.

"God, I'm gonna cum!" Priscilla said suddenly and she started rubbing her clit like crazy. Bob kicked it into high gear. In and out, he thrusted as her body began to shake. The rhythm of his thrusts matched that of her moans as she squirted all over his dick.

After she was finished, he decided that he couldn't hold it any more, so he pulled out. Priscilla eagerly took it in her mouth and began to suck as he started to cum. Bob always came huge amounts and today was no exception. She clamped her lips around his dick and began to gulp his semen as he pumped the massive load into her mouth. She didn't waste as single drop.

Jenny glanced over and was relieved that none had fallen onto her new carpet. But then she noticed that Priscilla had squirted everywhere. She couldn't help but reach down and start rubbing her pussy at the thought of it.

After witnessing the major fucking going on between her husband and Priscilla, Jenny picked up the pace and started bucking against Hal like a wild animal. He responded in kind and began fucking her so hard that she thought her fillings in her teeth were going to come loose. She loved to be fucked hard like this and started to cum instantly.

"Harder! You motherfucker!" She screamed and reached back and slapped Hal on the ass. "C'mon!"

Hal picked up the pace and began to really give her even harder. Pretty soon she settled down and he knew that she was finished. He decided to go ahead and cum.

"Where do you want it, Jenny?"

Jenny looked back at him and grinned. "I want it in my pussy. I want you to fill me full!"

Hal ejaculated deep into Jenny's vagina as he pumped her. He felt like he hadn't cum in ages as he filled her full to the rim. After he pulled out, he reached down and scooped up a couple of fingers' worth. Jenny grabbed his hand and sucked the semen off. She reached down and got some herself and began to eat it as she masturbated herself to another orgasm with the other hand.

Hal grinned, but then he saw the television again. Reminded of what he had seen earlier, his face fell. He looked over at Priscilla and saw that she had the same expression. Behind her, Bob poured gin and tonics for everyone. They were definitely going to need a drink.

"We're gonna have to do something," Priscilla said and lit a cigarette. "About Josie."

"Why don't you two go out there?" Jenny said and went over to Priscilla.

"Yeah, you could go out there and try to talk some sense into her," Bob said as he handed everyone their drinks.

"But she'll hate us, don't you think?" Priscilla said.

Hal put his head in his hand. "I knew we should have told her about us. About the *Lifestyle*. Maybe she wouldn't have done this."

"Oh, c'mon, Hal," Jenny said and took a sip of her drink. "You don't know that."

"At least if she had joined a cult, we could have her deprogrammed," Hal said.

Bob got a quizzical expression on his face. "Who says you can't still do that?"

"What do you mean, Bob?" Priscilla said, growing interested.

"Well, we could all fly out there and talk to her. We could tell her about our Lifestyle and how joining a religious group like that will ruin her career…"

Hal snapped his fingers. "Her career. Yeah, that's it. She loves being a porno actress. She obviously hasn't thought this thing through otherwise she would know that those people are going to make her stop."

Jenny chimed in, "Yeah, you can tell her about swinging and how it's ok to fuck other people and maybe she'll see just how crazy this religion stuff is."

Priscilla got a very determined expression on her face. "That does it. We're all flying out tomorrow and we're going to deprogram her."

"I'll book the flight right now," Bob said.

"If she could just see what she's doing with her life," Hal said, wringing his hands.

"Well, I guess we need to get packed," Jenny said and stood up.

"Jenny, one thing, don't forget your double-headed dildo," Priscilla said.

Jenny gave her an odd look. "Priscilla, this is your daughter we're talking about, remember?"

Priscilla rolled her eyes. "It's not for her. It's for us. I know I'm gonna have to relieve some tension before this is over."

16

As she was ushered back though the winding, utilitarian-looking hallway to Brother Red's office, Josie could feel herself growing so excited that she was about to jump out of her skin. She was so wet she was dripping. The thought of being alone in a room with Brother Red and his massive cock was just almost too much to think about.

Meanwhile, Red sat in his office, awaiting Josie's visit with so much excitement that his tight pants were about to split from the enormous hard-on he was sporting. He absently-minded stroked his penis through his pants, fantasizing about Josie wearing the black bra and panties. He was truly in love with her and he couldn't wait to give her the fucking of her life. He picked up a cream-filled doughnut from a box on his desk. He bit in and wondered if it was too soon to propose. After all, that was his ultimate goal. He had been with scads of women and had never been moved to such an extent as he had by watching Josie's movies. He just hoped that his brain would be able to function once he saw her in real life. Josie was the red-headed slut of his dreams and he did not want to blow it. He didn't, for one moment, doubt that she would be the wanton woman he so desired.

Red was just finishing his doughnut when Josie knocked on his door. He hurried up and swallowed. He checked himself in the mirror before he got the door.

"Hello, Miss Bistro," Red said coolly as he opened the door.

Josie's breath was taken away. Brother Red was even more good looking than she remembered and that cock! It was so huge! He was making no attempt to hide his hard-on.

"Hello..." Josie hesitated. She didn't know how exactly to address a man of Brother Red's stature.

"Just call me Red," Red laughed. "Please come in and have a seat."

Josie giggled and went in. Red bit his lip when Josie walked past him. Her ass was just so scrumptious that he could feel himself almost on the verge of cumming just from looking at it.

Josie sat down in a comfortable leather chair across from his desk. Red sat down on the desk in front her.

"Do you want a doughnut?" Red offered her the box.

Josie declined. "No, thanks, I just ate."

Red placed the doughnuts back down on the desk and was suddenly at a loss for words. What can you say when the woman of your dreams walks through your door? Josie nervously looked around the room for a few seconds not knowing if she was going to be kicked out of the church or what. She noticed that the office was decorated with ancient scrolls and also some phallic looking fertility statues. She was impressed. Finally, Red realized that he had to say something or he was definitely going to lose her attention.

"Miss Bistro..." Red began.

"You can call me Josie," Josie giggled. "I don't mind."

Red almost swooned.

"Josie," he smiled. "You're probably wondering why I asked you to come here."

"Sorta."

"Well, one of the reasons is that I really appreciate all the work you're doing for the church. You are, indeed, a blessing."

"Thanks, Red," Josie beamed. "I love helping out. I tell you, coming to the Cardboard Cathedral has been one the best things that's ever happened to me."

"Thank you, sister. Thank you," Red said and leaned in a little closer to her. He got a better look at her cleavage and his hard-on jumped. It was almost too much just looking at her bra and panties through her see-through dress, but this was something else entirely. Josie breathing sped up as his still hard monster dick moved closer to her. "Actually, there's another reason I wanted you to come to my office."

Before he had a chance to say anything, Josie suddenly got a thought.

"You don't want me to quit being a porno actress do you?" Josie blurted out, her heart sinking. She didn't know what she would do if he asked her to do that. She had asked Sister Gwen this question before, but for some reason, was never satisfied with her answers. She wanted to find out from the man himself.

Red started chuckling. "No, no, sister. We've got room for everybody here. No, it's nothing like that at all." Red smiled. "It's just that..." Red hesitated. "I think you are absolutely the most beautiful woman I have ever seen and I would love it if you would go out with me tonight."

Josie's breath was taken away. She just couldn't believe her ears. Brother Red Hair and his cock had just asked her out!

Without hesitating or even giving it any thought, Josie answered, "I would love it!"

Red burst into a smile and almost started dancing around the room. He was so happy. Josie, on the other hand, couldn't keep her eyes off his massive penis. It was like it was mesmerizing her to a point where she felt like she was yearning for it. Before she realized it, she found herself talking.

"But only on one condition."

Red's smile fell. What if she wanted something that he couldn't possibly give her? Surely, it wasn't supposed to end this way?

"You've got to let me have a taste of that big cock of yours," Josie said before she thought about it.

Red looked at her a bit strangely. "You want what?" He said and broke into a grin.

Josie put her hand over her mouth. Surely, she didn't just say that.

"Oh, I'm so sorry! I can't believe I just said that! Please forget what I just said! I'm a porno actress, remember? I just can't keep my filthy mouth shut!" Josie was so embarrassed that wanted to run from the room.

Red leaned in close to her and started rubbing her breasts.

"I think I can meet your condition," he said and started nuzzling her neck. Josie moaned as her hands immediately went to Red's zipper. The big dick sprung out of his pants and she had in her mouth in no time. She got down on her knees and started sucking for all she was worth. Red again looked down her top at her tits, still encased in her black bra and felt himself starting to lose control. He put his mind on something else and began to push her head down, driving his cock down her throat. He was there fast. At the first taste of Red's salty pre-cum, Josie began to finger her already wet pussy through her panties. She orgasmed within seconds and was well on her way to another one when Red gently took his dick out of her mouth and hoisted her up onto his desk and began to eat her out. She came again as he began to munch on her delicious pussy. His face was soon coated with her juice, but he kept licking and sucking and driving her crazy. He stuck one finger up her ass as he licked. While she loved the way he ate pussy, she really wanted to have that big dick of his inside of her.

"C'mon, Red, fuck me," she moaned breathily as she rolled over onto her stomach.

He stood up and gently put it in, going just an inch at a time until he was finally all the way in. He was amazed that such a little girl was able to take his full eleven inches so easily. There had been very few that could.

Looking down at her sweet ass and at her beautiful tits squashed down on the desk top, Red was inspired to start fucking her hard. She looked like she needed a good hard fucking. It was what she was used to. Anything less than a ferocious pounding would be a letdown to a girl like her. He almost started cumming just thinking about all the men that she had been with and how easily that she allowed men to fuck her. His dream girl was a slut and he couldn't have been happier.

"Give it to me, Red! Harder!" Josie moaned as she convulsed with another orgasm. She bucked against him harder and harder until he was certain that they were actually moving the heavy mahogany desk. He threw it into high gear. After that, he couldn't stand it anymore.

"I'm gonna cum!"

Josie got down on her knees and started giving him head. She licked the tip of his big cock until he finally squirted all into her mouth and all over her face. As she wiped the sperm from her face with her fingers, she realized that she had never seen a man cum so much. She licked her fingers and realized that Red not only had an enormous cock, but he also was full of cum. How did she get so lucky? She asked herself.

Red sat down on his desk and lit a cigarette for himself and Josie. As they smoked, they just looked at each other and couldn't stop smiling.

"Are you sure you don't want a doughnut?" Red asked again.

"Thanks, Red. I've changed my mind. I think I would like one."

17

Brother Farlin lit up a cigarette in the hallway that contained the church offices. He was pretty aggravated. He had just finished talking to that guy, Gunter, and was now a little pissed off. How dare that guy think that he would betray the only man who had ever given him a chance just for a little pocket money and revenge.

"That guy deserves to burn in hell," Brother Farlin mumbled to himself as he walked past Brother Red's office. He had taken his Viagra in anticipation of banging the girls, but, for some reason, had not been invited to the activity. He thought for a second about knocking on Brother Red's door, but then realized that it probably wasn't a good idea. That girl, Josie, was something special to him. While he knew that Brother Red might not mind sharing her, he thought it best to wait until the girl was actually presented to them. He didn't want to be rude or anything. He knew that Red would start sharing her eventually. He couldn't help but feel a small twinge in his penis and lick his lips in anticipation.

He walked on down the hall, ashing his cigarette in a potted plant. His hard-on was aching at the thought of Josie getting fucked by Brother Red. He could just imagine her clawing the floors while she was getting it hard from behind. He just couldn't hardly stand it. He started rubbing himself through his pants. He then heard some animal-like grunting coming from the office directly in front of him. He paused for a second and then realized that Brother Abernathy and Brother Myrtlewood were servicing Marcy! How could he have forgotten that? Now, that girl was a real piece of ass. He guessed it was because that guy Gunter was muddling his mind. What kind of a person did that guy take him for, anyway? That guy didn't know him. He wasn't even an American for goodness sake!

He walked into the office and was pleasantly surprised to see Marcy being sandwiched by Brother Abernathy and Brother Myrtlewood. Brother Abernathy was dogging her and Brother Myrtlewood had his dick stuck deep down into her throat. Her enormous breasts heaved with every thrust she gave and took. Her leg muscles were taut as she received her pounding from Brother Abernathy.

Brother Farlin couldn't help but break into a smile. His erection was already straining his pants. It begged for release. He started taking his pants off when Brother Abernathy noticed him.

"Yo, Farlin, go get the camera, man! We've got to go get some pictures of this."

"Yeah, man, get the pictures! This girl is crazy!" Brother Myrtlewood turned and chimed in. Marcy almost started laughing, but was unable to due to the large dick in her mouth.

"Oh, we don't need the camera, do we?" Brother Farlin almost whined. "I want to get some too."

Marcy looked up and took the dick out of her mouth long enough to talk. "C'mon, Brother Farlin, take some pictures. You can jerk off while we fuck. I love to see a man jerk off while I'm getting fucked." Then she suddenly started bucking against Brother Abernathy as she had a monstrous orgasm.

"I think I'm losing my mind!" she said as she came.

Brother Abernathy picked up the pace and started really long-stroking her. "You heard her, man! Go get it!"

Brother Farlin just stood there and started rubbing his dick. Then he decided to go get the camera.

A couple of seconds after he had left, Brother Myrtlewood pulled out of her mouth.

"I can't stand it no more!" He said and started shooting his load all over her face and tits. She opened her mouth and lapped up the cum like she hadn't had anything to eat in days. Brother Abernathy almost lost it when she began licking the semen off her breasts.

"C'mon, hurry up, Brother Abernathy, I want some of that black cum on me too!" Marcy said breathlessly as she turned around.

"Yeah, baby!"

Brother Abernathy pulled out and unloaded into her waiting mouth.

Brother Farlin came back with the camera a couple of minutes later. He started masturbating again and then noticed that everyone was sitting around smoking cigarettes. He also noticed that Marcy was coated in cum.

"You're too late, brother. You missed it," Brother Abernathy said as he took a long drag off his Kool.

"I'm sorry," Marcy said sheepishly. "I really wanted to give you a good show. We just got too worked up."

Brother Farlin put the camera down and stood there for a minute, stroking his hard-on but not really getting anything out of it. He was a little miffed that they hadn't waited on him. He thought for a second and walked out. He didn't want to say anything that he might regret later. He walked down the hallway, hard-on in hand, wondering how in the world that his so-called friends could be so rude to him. He didn't ask for much. He just wanted to get a piece of the action too. He was on the verge of getting depressed when all of a sudden he heard some moans coming out of Sister Gwen's office. That was good news. Sister Gwen was a real party girl and would fuck almost anything that moved. Maybe she would be able to do something about his aching hard-on.

He opened the door quietly, hoping maybe to get a glimpse of the action before anyone knew he was there. He slipped in unnoticed and was astounded by what he saw. Sister Gwen was on the one side of a double-headed dildo with a girl, who from her moans, sounded English. It was one of the new girls, Vanessa Perkins. His penis really stood to attention when he saw Sister Gwen's face buried in a beautiful Latina's pussy. It was the other new girl, Carmen. Sister Gwen was showing them the ropes all right.

Sister Gwen was really munching too. Carmen sat in an office chair and had her fingers buried deep in her hair and held her head tight as she hunched against her face. Vanessa soon pulled the double-headed dildo out. She licked it first and then began eating Sister Gwen. It was a daisy chain. Vanessa ate vigorously, and fingered her own pussy while she licked. The girls moaning occasionally reached feverish pitches as they came.

Brother Farlin stood there for a second really giving it all he had, feeling the semen welling up inside of him. As he watched the girls having sex, it was almost overwhelming for him. The smell of pussy was just so strong. He stepped out into the room, hard-on displayed for the girls to see. He had to have a piece and he had to have it now!

Vanessa screamed when she saw him.

"AAAAhhhh! Who's that pervert!"

Carmen jumped about a mile off the chair and Sister Gwen quickly turned to see what was the matter.

"Brother Farlin! You shouldn't be sneaking around like that!"

"I just couldn't help myself."

"You know him?" Carmen said, pointing at him like he was some sort of thing, rather than a person.

Sister Gwen quickly explained who Brother Farlin was and the girls breathed a sigh of relief. Pretty soon, they were getting frisky again and Brother Farlin moved in closer to the action. Maybe he would be able to get some from Sister Gwen at least.

As he started sucking on Sister Gwen's sweaty tits, she sat up.

"I've got a great idea!" She turned to Brother Farlin. "Why don't you go get the camera?"

Brother Farlin looked at her like he could've fallen through the floor.

"That's a brilliant idea!" Vanessa chimed in.

Carmen nodded her head enthusiastically.

Brother Farlin looked at them and then sighed. He picked up his pants and walked out the door and towards his office. He wasn't going to get the camera, however he was going to make a phone call.

18

"Gosh, I just don't know if I can believe all this," Josie said as she sat across from Red at the Chateau Gourmet that Sunday night. It had once been one of the swankiest eateries in Red's part of Los Angeles. It was decorated with heavy drapes and dark wood and had been around since the forties with little or no remodeling. Some people might have called it a dump but to Red it was very stylish. It had a lot of character, he thought. Looking over at Josie in her sheer black dress, he was still amazed at how lucky he was.

"C'mon, Josie. Surely, it doesn't blow you away you that much," Red said as he took a sip of his wine. He wasn't even looking over his shoulder as he drank. He usually did this to watch for snoops sent out by the other televangelists. It was a very cutthroat business and he always had to be on his toes. If any one of them saw him drink or be out with a girl like Josie, it would be reported directly to their superiors and the war would be on. This was especially true of his arch rival, the Reverend Simon Pure. That guy was always trying to get him on something.

"But, Red, you're a preacher! Preachers don't go around screwing anyone they want to. It's like you're a...swinger or something."

Red had opened up and told Josie about his philosophy of free love and how one shouldn't be ashamed to get down and freaky however and with whomever one likes. Josie, needless to say, was a little taken aback. She had never met a preacher like this before. She didn't know what to think, but she was thinking that she liked it.

"Josie, I believe that sex between two or more consenting adults is a beautiful thing. It's just people being people. Besides, it's just fun. I don't see anything morally wrong with it all."

Josie looked at him over her lobster for a minute and then smiled.

"So, is that why you don't mind me being a porno actress?"

Red smiled. "Well, sort of, but there's more..." He debated with himself for a moment whether or not to tell her his dream. It was early and it was only their first date. He decided against it. There would be time later. "I just think that you're a great porno actress and it would be a shame for you not to do something you love and are good at."

Josie swallowed her lobster and took a sip of wine. "You're right about that. I love it. Getting fucked by guy or girl I've only known for a few minutes is one of the biggest turn-ons I can think of." Josie paused and thought for a second. "So, you really don't mind that I'm porno actress? I'm not talking about the church, I'm talking about...as far as we're concerned."

Red smiled. "I just want you to be happy."

Josie smiled and took another bite of lobster.

After they finished dinner, Red drove Josie around to some of his charities. Most were in the rougher parts of town. They were usually in partially abandoned strip malls and shopping centers. They drove by thrift stores, soup kitchens and literacy centers.

"Wow, you do so much good, Red. It's such a turn-on to be around somebody who impacts so many people's lives."

"I'm just an instrument. Remember that. If I don't help people, I don't think that I'm doing what I'm supposed to be doing." This was probably the most true thing about Red. He always believed in sharing. Whether it came to his money or his women, what was his was everybody else's. Everybody deserved a piece. While he realized that he was a little over the top and sometimes acted as though he had a little more power than he really did, he also realized what he did was for the greater good. If people bought it and it made their lives a little easier, then so be it.

"That's so sweet," Josie said and gave him a little kiss. She rubbed his crotch through his pants and was pleased to see that he was already hard. She lingered on the head for a minute, still amazed at its enormity.

"There's another place I want to show you," Red said and did a u-turn

He drove for a couple of minutes, deeper into the bad part of town.

"It's just up there." Red pointed up ahead at a lighted building. It was the only building with lights in the whole deserted industrial block. Besides the building, there was nothing on the street but abandoned warehouses and train tracks. They pulled up to it and parked on the street, in front of it.

"It's a mission house," Josie said.

"Yep, this is where I started out. This is the birthplace of the Cardboard Cathedral, even before there was a *Church of What's Happenin' Now.*"

When they walked in, they were greeted to lots of "hellos" and handshakes. People gathered around Red like moths to a flame. There were old people, young people and all sorts of people in between. Josie was very impressed, even though it saddened her to see the poverty etched on the people's faces. Regardless, it was easy to see that these people loved Red. The place was just a big room filled with cots and only had a small kitchen. Still, though, it was the only home that some of them had known for years.

A big, long haired Mexican looking guy wearing an apron walked up to Red and gave him a hug.

"Red! It's so good to see you, brother!"

Red hugged him back. "This here is Brother Juan. He runs the place."

Brother Juan extended his hand. As Josie took it, she couldn't help but notice what a stud he was. He was muscular and she could see everything through his tight jeans. He was hung like a horse. Not as big as Red, but still, who was?

"Pleased to meet you," Juan said. "Any friend of Red's is a friend of mine." Just then there was a little ruckus in the back of the mission. "If you'll excuse me for a second, I have to go take care of some trouble." He walked quickly to the back for a second. It appeared that a midget was wrestling with an old woman for a cot.

"Juan here was one of the worst crack heads I've ever seen. But he's really straightened himself up and now he's in charge of the place."

"Wow, that's great," Josie said.

"All he needed was a chance," Red said.

Josie looked at Red for a second. "Red, I want to help. What can I do?"

Red looked at her for a minute. "Well, I'm sure Juan needs some help in the kitchen. Maybe we could go back there..."

"But I'm no good in the kitchen!" Josie whined. "I'm no good at anything."

Red thought for a second and smiled. "Well, you are good at something, you know."

Josie thought for a second and smiled.

She grabbed Red by the hand and walked to the kitchen. Brother Juan came in few seconds later.

"Man, that midget is always starting something!" Brother Juan said and washed his hands.

"Juan, I want to help," Josie said and moved in close to him.

"Well..." Brother Juan said at a loss for words. "I don't really need..."

"No, Juan, she insists," Red said and smiled and started rubbing Josie's ass.

Brother Juan smiled as Josie pulled his penis out of his pants. She got down on her knees and clamped her lips onto the head. He grew hard as she sucked and within seconds he was fully upright. Red pulled out his dick and began to rub it. It had been hard all night and it felt good to finally give it a little attention. He lifted up Josie's skirt and was a little disappointed to see that she wasn't wearing any panties. Still, an ass like that was nothing to sneeze at.

She unbuttoned her dress as she sucked and pushed it down around her waist. She was wearing a black bra. Delighted, Red almost moaned at the sight of it. He got down and began to lick her pussy as she sucked Juan's dick. She tasted great and was so wet that she was dripping onto the floor. Soon, his face was glazed over. He couldn't wait any longer. The sight of the woman of his dreams slutting herself out to another man was just too much for him. He pulled down his pants and put his big dick in her. She shuddered with excitement as he began to stroke her doggie style. Red was amazed. He hadn't even started fucking her good yet and she had already had an orgasm. She continued to suck Brother Juan and soon she could taste the pre-cum. She began to rub her tits and the combination of the taste and Red's hammering her pussy, she came again. Red really started pumping her then. Brother Juan had hard time fighting the urge to cum, but somehow he managed.

"I've got to fuck you in the ass, girl!" Brother Juan said breathily.

"I would love that!" Josie said as she took a breath.

Red smiled and changed places with Juan. This time Josie was on all fours and giving head to Red while Brother Juan began to insert his dick into her anus. He rubbed her pussy as he did it. At first, he thought that it might be a little tight, but to his surprise, he slid right in.

"Damn! This girl is off the hook!" Brother Juan said happily and began to ream her.

Josie laughed and then started deepthroating Red. After a little bit of Juan's pounding she had the biggest orgasm of the night. Anal orgasms were always big for her but this time, she almost drew blood from Red's legs she was clawing them so hard. She was lucky that her screams of ecstasy didn't bring draw an audience.

After she had finished shaking and convulsing, it was all that Red could take. He pulled out and shot cum all over her face and in her mouth. Before she even had a chance to lick it up, Brother Juan came with a shudder all over her ass.

Josie wiped up the cum and licked her fingers clean.

Brother Juan just looked at her in amazement. "You can come and help me anytime!" He laughed and high-fived Red.

Josie just laughed, but couldn't help but notice the odd smile on Red's face. She didn't know it, but he was the happiest man on Earth at that moment. He had also decided to tell her about his dream.

19

"God, I've got to have a cigarette!" Priscilla said after their plane landed in Atlanta. They had a two hour layover before the second leg of their flight to Los Angeles took off.

Jenny gave Priscilla an odd look. "You don't smoke!"

"After a flight like that I do," Priscilla said as they trucked their way into the concourse. The turbulence had been so bad that, at one point, Priscilla's head had bumped the overhead bin.

"It was great that we were able to get these tickets on such short notice," Hal said, hustling to keep up with Priscilla.

"Don't be too thankful. We did have to stop in Atlanta," Bob said.

"Oh yeah."

They hurried along and finally went into a smoking lounge that adjoined a bar. Bob and Hal went to buy some beer while the girls lit up.

"I only hope that we're not too late," Priscilla said, savoring the Marlboro Ultra Light. It was the first one she had had in over five years. It was a little harsh but it tasted good.

"I'm sure we're not. Josie's a smart girl. She can make up her own mind."

"I hope so," Priscilla exhaled.

After a few minutes the guys came back with the beers. Everyone was so thirsty, that the beers looked like about most refreshing things in the world. After about half a glass, the girls began feeling a little tipsy.

"You're not gonna believe this but I think I'm feeling a little drunk," Jenny said.

"You and me both," Priscilla said.

Bob and Hal laughed and talked about the news that was showing on the smoke room's television.

Jenny looked around the smoking lounge. There weren't a lot of people, just a few workers and some foreigners. Then she looked at Priscilla slyly. She moved her chair closer to her.

"What are you doing?" Priscilla said.

"Ssshh," Jenny said as she slipped her hand up Priscilla's denim skirt. She found her mark within seconds and began to gently massage Priscilla's pussy.

"Mmmm…" Pricilla moaned. "What are you doing?"

"I'm relieving some of your stress." Jenny said as she kept rubbing. After Priscilla was good and juicy, she licked her fingers, but not before offering them to Priscilla who eagerly tasted herself.

Bob nudged Hal and pointed over to the girls. Hal couldn't help but start grinning. Only someone who was actually paying attention to them could have been able to see what was going on. It just looked like the two women were sitting together. Bob and Hal blocked any clear view of what was going on.

Jenny slipped three fingers into her pussy and began to gently finger fuck her. She moved them in a small circular movement. This clearly did the trick. Priscilla writhed and after a few minutes began to cum. She stifled the urge to cry out in ecstasy. However, she did cum with an enormous shudder.

After she came, she lit a cigarette and gave Jenny a deep french-kiss.

"Me next," Hal joked to Jenny.

"Well, come on over and let's get started," Jenny said.

"Shut up," Priscilla said suddenly.

Everyone at the table gave her an odd look. Surely, she wasn't picking this moment to be jealous.

"I didn't offend you by saying that to him did I?" Jenny asked nervously.

"No. Don't be silly. Look," Priscilla said and pointed at the TV.

They all turned and looked at the screen. The smiling face of Brother Red Hair filled the screen. It was a report about an alleged sex scandal at the Cardboard Cathedral.

Red's little secret was out. All the tales and pictures of his debaucheries had hit the news. The report mentioned that he was into group sex, prostitution, porn and many other sexual perversions. Of course, most of what was being said was pure fabrication, but it's irrelevant to most people whether or not something is true or not, just that somebody says it. Especially when it comes to the subject of sex. The reporter even spoke to Red's rival, the Reverend Simon Pure.

"This man deserves nothing less than hell!" The Reverend Pure thundered as his face turned red and the veins popped out in his head. "The problem today is that there's no accountability! There's no consequences! Well, there's gonna be consequences in hell for Red Hair, I can guarantee that!"

"We've got to hurry," Priscilla said. "There's no telling what kind of depraved person Josie has decided to follow."

"Why that pervert!" Hal said. "Just wait until I get my hands on him!"

20

"I...just...don't know what to say." Josie was speechless. She was lying nude on Red's bed, trying to keep her legs from turning to jelly. She smoked a cigarette and focused her attention on Red's giant cock which was still semi-hard even after having sex with her all night.

Red's mansion was out in the suburbs. It was an extravagant house that had once belonged to some silent movie mogul who had gotten into trouble for being married to three women at the same time. It was gigantic and Red had decorated it so that it was more suited for European royalty than it was a fundamentalist preacher from Texas. It was very high on the gilt and velvet and very low on the modesty. It was like Elvis Presley and Marilyn Monroe had run amok.

"Don't say anything. I just wanted you to know just how special you are to me," Red said. He focused on her gorgeous breasts in an effort not to appear too nervous. He had just told her his dream about them being married. He had told her everything from the gangbang to the black bra and panties. He had told her how much he loved slutty women and exactly how much she meant to him. He had been extremely nervous about doing it, but he felt that he had to. He was just so happy and he wanted her to know that she was the one for him.

"That's just so romantic," Josie said, reaching out and stroking Red's cock with her free hand. The other hand ashed the cigarette into an ornate jade ashtray that Red had picked up on one of his many crusades to Southeast Asia. She just didn't know what to say. She was so moved that she almost wanted to burst into tears. As far as she knew she had never been the girl of anyone's dreams. Then she remembered that she was a porno actress and realized that she probably had the girl of many people's fantasies, but, regardless, she had hit the jackpot with this one. To be the girl of a great man like the Brother Red Hair's dreams was something she had never thought possible. It was like she was Cinderella or something. It was like the man of her dreams had picked her. It was overwhelming. Her eyes began to well up with tears.

Red moved in close and kissed her. "What's wrong? I didn't scare you or anything, did I?"

"Red," Josie said, breaking into a smile, her eyes still teary. "That's the sweetest thing anything anyone has ever said to me. I'm so lucky to have you."

Red was so happy. His dreams had come true and his prayers had been answered. He leaned over and began to kiss Josie deeply. She kissed him back and began to gently stroke his penis. He stiffened instantly. He reached down and began to rub her pussy. It was still a little raw from the workout he had given her earlier, but she was already wet to the touch.

"Red, let's skip all this stuff and get down to the fucking," Josie said breathily as he put his fingers into her. Her breasts heaved up and down in her excitement.

Red broke into a smile. He leaned Josie back and started to enter her missionary style.

"No, Red, I want you to do me doggie," Josie said, rolling over onto her stomach and getting up on all fours.

Red couldn't help but smile again. He loved fucking Josie doggie style. He loved watching her leaning in to him and grabbing the sheets. He began ramming her from the get go. Thrusting deeply into her, she moaned with every stroke.

"Really fuck me hard, Red. I need it," she moaned.

Red really started pumping her then, grabbing her hips and pulling her back onto him with each thrust. Josie came after only a few seconds of this. After shuddering for a few seconds she got into a groove where she was really bucking into him hard. Red had never felt so good fucking a girl.

"I wish you had two dicks, Red. I would love to be sucking a cock right now," Josie said breathily. Since hearing about Red's dream, she was turned on more than ever. Especially since she knew that he loved hearing her talk like that. Red had a hard time fighting back the cum after her comment.

Red was really pounding her when all of a sudden, the bedroom door burst open.

It was Sister Gwen.

"Brother Red, I'm sorry to interrupt…" She looked at Josie whose eyes had almost rolled back into her head with ecstasy and winked. "…but you're not gonna believe what they're talking about on TV."

She flicked on the TV before he had a chance to answer.

Red slowed down to a slower pace as he watched the breaking news about the "perverted pastor" as they were now calling him. He watched with a slight revulsion as the Rev. Simon Pure blustered about his moral depravity.

"Well," Red sighed as he continued to slowly fuck Josie. "I guess the cat's out of the bag."

"So, what are we gonna do, Brother Red? What about the Church? This is gonna kill it," she said nervously. She fidgeted from leg to leg as Josie stared her squarely in the eye as she was being fucked. Sister Gwen was getting wet fast.

"I don't know what to do, Gwen. I really don't," Red said.

Sister Gwen couldn't keep her attention off Josie. Her eyes were almost glazed over in lust as she nodded to Red.

"Well, I know what Sister Gwen can do," Josie said, pushing hard against Red. "She can get her clothes off and come over here and join us."

Sister Gwen smiled. "That sounds like a pretty good plan."

She quickly slipped out of her skirt and top and got on the bed with them. Red pumped Josie even harder as she pulled Sister Gwen over to her and began to lick her already wet pussy. Sister Gwen moaned in ecstasy as Josie's experienced lips and fingers explored her. Josie came again as Red picked up the pace and fucked her with wild abandon.

"Let's switch. I want you to fuck her while she eats my pussy," Josie said.

"Great idea!" Sister Gwen said. "I love Red's big cock."

The girls switched out and soon he was pounding Sister Gwen and slapping her ass while she ate Josie's pussy. Sister Gwen came fast from the fucking because Josie had already gotten her heated up. Josie came again from the cunnilingus.

After a bit, Red pulled out. "Girls, I just can't take it anymore."

"Well, don't waste it!" Josie said and started sucking his dick. Sister Gwen got down and helped her with it. After a few seconds, Red squirted a big thick load all over the both of them. They licked each other's faces clean and then shared a kiss.

As they all sat around afterwards, smoking cigarettes. Red told Sister Gwen all about him and Josie.

"That's so great! I just wish all this other stuff hadn't happened."

"I know," Red said.

"So, Red, what can you do?" Josie said. "Do you think that you can deny it?"

"I don't think so. I mean if they've got the pictures…"

"But what I want to know is how can they even have the pictures…?" Sister Gwen said.

Just then the sound of helicopters became overwhelming.

"What's that?" Sister Gwen said and jumped off the bed. She ran over to the window and looked out.

"It's a helicopter and it's…"

"It's filming you!" Josie cried and pointed at the television. Sure enough, there on the news was Sister Gwen looking out of the window nude. Her breasts and pubic area were blurred but there she was.

Red got up and looked out the window. He appeared on TV too. As naked as a jaybird. He took a look around his property.

"There are reporters everywhere," he said softly. News crews were parked all up and down his street. He walked back to the bed and lay down beside Josie.

"I'm screwed," he said. "I'll never preach again."

Josie shook her head and began to cry.

"Don't say that, Red. You're too good a person for that. You help too many people."

Sister Gwen came over and joined them.

"Yeah, Red, Josie's right. You can't give up. There's got to be a way."

Red shook his head.

"If I had stolen from my congregation like Simon Asshole Pure, they wouldn't even care. But let me have a little sex and it's the end of the world."

"I would just like to know who did this to you," Sister Gwen said. "You've never hurt anybody."

"Maybe I deserve it," Red said. "For living one way and acting another."

"Nobody deserves this," Josie said. "If I could just get my hands on the person who did this…"

"No, Josie, we shouldn't wish this person harm. I'm sure they had their reasons," Red said. "I just wish they would have come to me first and maybe we could have worked something out."

21

"We did good, baby," Gunter said as he took a bite of his club sandwich. "You got your revenge and a little money for your pain and suffering."

Brother Farlin sat directly across from him. While he had ordered a cheeseburger and fries, he found that he wasn't really that hungry. In fact, he hadn't been hungry since the news hit.

"I can't believe that I listened to you. Red was my friend and I betrayed him because of you. Who are you anyway? You're nothing to me." Brother Farlin hung his head in his hands. "I wish I was dead."

Gunter chuckled. "It's ok, baby. You're just forgetting that that he's the guy who wasn't sharing his pussy with you. He didn't look out for your needs. He deserved it, keeping all that sweet pussy to himself."

Brother Farlin nervously lit up a cigarette. "But that's not really true. I did get laid sometimes. It's just…" He tried to ash the cigarette and only managed to break it in the process. "…oh, I don't know! I'm such a fool!" He put his head in his hands again.

Gunter rolled his eyes. "You've got to grow some balls, baby. Especially, if you're going to go on the talk shows and talk about what a pervert that guy is. You don't want to miss out on that kind of money."

"Talk shows?" Brother Farlin looked up.

"Oh, yes, baby. I've already booked you on several." Gunter smiled back. He had big plans for Brother Farlin. He would do the talk show circuit, the lecture circuit, the religious circuit and then the high school circuit. He would not only be able to get his Audi fixed with the money that would be rolling in, he would also be able to buy several new ones as well. This was one of the best ideas that he had ever had.

"You? Wha...?"

"Oh, I'm your manager, now, baby. I hope you don't mind. I just thought that you would want to...how you say...make hay while the sun is shining."

Brother Farlin emphatically shook his head. "I don't want any of this. I wish I had never met you."

"Well, you did, so let's make the most of it."

Brother Farlin narrowed his eyes at Gunter. "And Brother Red is not a pervert. Not any more so than you, anyway."

"Well, what is he then, baby?"

"He's my friend."

"*Was* your friend, baby. Now, he's your cash cow."

Brother Farlin sat there for a moment. He lit another cigarette. "No, this is gonna stop."

A worried look crossed Gunter's face. "Don't do something stupid now. This is a going to be a good thing for the both of us. Let's make lemonade out of this lemon, okay, baby?"

Brother Farlin shook his head slowly.

"No, we're not." He looked up at Gunter. "I'm sorry if I said anything mean to you, about being a foreigner and all. I know you can't help it."

"That's okay. I am a foreigner. I admit it," Gunter said and smiled, though it was hard because he could see all his dreams rapidly going down the drain.

"And I'm sorry for saying that I wish that I had never met you. You can't help the way you are. Brother Red says that there's room for everybody. We just have to open our hearts enough so they'll fit."

Now, it was Gunter's turn to shake his head. "No, baby..."

"Yes, Gunter. I'm going to Brother Red and ask for forgiveness. I know I don't deserve it, but I can't let everything that man has done for me slide down the tubes."

"But what has he done for you, lately?" Gunter said harshly, almost spitting across the table. He couldn't understand how Brother Farlin could be so stupid. How he could just throw away all this money? But he also realized that maybe money wasn't everything to a guy like Brother Farlin. It hurt his stomach to even think this.

"Goodbye, Gunter. You're welcome to come with me if you want."

Gunter stared at him.

"Brother Red is a very forgiving person."

For the first time, Gunter began to feel a twinge of guilt. "No, I can't. I have to get my Audi out of the shop."

22

"Man, we came as soon as we heard," Brother Abernathy said as he greeted Red, Josie and Sister Gwen at the door of the Cardboard Cathedral. They had had a hard time fighting their way through the crowd of reporters and protesters. Many of the protesters were followers of Rev. Pure. They held up signs up with slogans such as, "Go back to hell, you Demon!" and "Pornography Kills." One of the signs that especially pained Red was one that attacked Josie. It said, "Preachers don't date sluts!"

While he was happy that Josie was indeed a slut, his interpretation of the word was something far different than what they meant. They spit at him and grabbed at him as had made his way through the mob. Red was lucky that he hadn't been torn apart.

Brother Abernathy's clothes were disheveled and looked like they had just been thrown on. Red took a look at the three half-dressed Thai hookers lounging around the reception area and realized the reason behind Brother Abernathy's appearance.

"Thanks, Brother," Red said shaking his hand. He was happy to see that Brother Abernathy was still on his side. It was good to see that it hadn't been him that had betrayed him.

Just then Brother Myrtlewood burst out of the TV production area.

"Brother Red, I've got everything set up. Whenever you're ready to tell your side of the story, we're ready. We can break into our regular programming and start broadcasting it immediately."

Brother Myrtlewood looked in a similar state of disarray as Brother Abernathy. He also smelled heavily of liquor and marijuana. His pants were also still unzipped and his semi-hard penis was hanging out. Marcy walked out of the production area a couple of seconds after him, wiping her mouth. It was obvious that he hadn't been the one who had betrayed him either.

Marcy walked over and gave Josie a big hug.

"Thanks, Brother Myrtlewood. Just give me a minute."

Red turned to Josie. "I'm sorry that you had to get dragged into this."

"I'm just glad that I'm here to help you through it," Josie said.

"So, what are you gonna do, Red? Deny it? I'm sure we can say the pics are fakes or something," Brother Myrtlewood said and lit up a cigarette.

Red shook his head. "No, I said that I'm not gonna do that. I can't lie about this. I've been lying for so long about this stuff. I'm tired of it. I don't feel anything is wrong with it. If I lie about or apologize for what I've done, then it'll be like I feel that it's wrong."

"You know that this is gonna kill your ministry, don't you?" Brother Abernathy said, barely unable to keep his eyes off Josie's hot little body.

"Probably. But I've got to stand up for what I believe in. This is something I've got to do."

Suddenly a commotion erupted behind them, at the door of the church.

"You pervert! Let go of our daughter!"

"Daddy!" Josie said as she saw her parents along with Bob and Jenny entering the building.

Hal and Bob rushed over to Red. Brother Abernathy tried to stop them but they pushed him aside. Before he knew it, Hal had knocked Red down to the ground.

"How dare you try to brainwash my little girl, you red headed woodpecker!"

"Hal, leave some for me," Bob said rolling up his sleeves.

"I'll show you what's happenin' now, you son of a bitch!" Hal said as he jumped on top of Red and punched him in the jaw.

"Bob!" Josie cried. "Please Daddy! Stop! Mom! You've got to make him stop! He's hurting Red!"

Priscilla walked over and put her arms around Josie.

"It's okay, Josie. It's normal for you to feel empathy for the man who brainwashed you," she said soothingly. She turned to Marcy. "I hope you haven't joined this cult, too."

"But it's not a cult!" Josie protested.

"Sure it is, dear. It's a cult run by a pervert." Priscilla took a look at Red who was still being held down by Hal. He was sitting on him and, as a prelude to beating him, lecturing him about how he shouldn't be brainwashing impressionable young girls. She could see the imprint of Red's gigantic penis through his pants and felt a little twinge. "I can easily see why a girl would get...overwhelmed by his..."

"But he's not a pervert! And it's not a cult! He's a swinger and he helps people. Daddy can't hurt him because I love him!" Josie exclaimed.

Priscilla let go of Josie.

"He's a..."

"He's a swinger, Mom. You know, he has sex with people. He's just like me, except he doesn't get paid for it. He never told anybody about it because he was afraid that people would stop supporting his church and he wouldn't be able to help anybody."

Priscilla's jaw dropped. She looked over at Jenny who was also dumbstruck.

"Hal! Bob! Come over here! You've got to hear this!"

Hal looked over his shoulder.

"I'm kinda in the middle of something here," Hal protested.

"He's a swinger," Jenny said.

Hal looked at Red and then looked at Priscilla who nodded her head. He got up off Red and walked over to Josie and Priscilla. Red stood up and dusted himself off. He rubbed his chin where Hal had socked him.

"So, he's a..."

"Yes, Daddy, he's a swinger, You know..."

"Honey, we know what swingers are." Hal looked at Priscilla and nodded her head slightly.

"Honey, there's something we need to tell you…" Hal said and took her hand.

Josie's jaw dropped as Hal told her all about how he and Priscilla were swingers and how Bob and Jenny were also swingers. He told her about their parties and conventions. Josie was stunned, but it did clear up a lot of things for her. For example, she had never understood how her parents could always be meeting so many new people and why they were always going to so many parties. And here she had thought that Mom and Dad were just a couple of squares. She was definitely going to have to rethink how she viewed them.

After he was finished, Hal had a few questions for her. "So, is everybody here…"

"I know Sister Gwen is and I think Brother Abernathy and Brother Myrtlewood are too. I don't know about Brother Farlin…"

"Brother Farlin!" Sister Gwen said and snapped her fingers. "I knew we were missing someone. I wonder what happened to him?"

"I think I know," Red said quietly. "He was the one."

"He was the one what?" Bob said.

"He was the one who betrayed me," Red said.

It was like a light was turned on in the minds of everyone there. They all knew beyond a shadow of doubt that he was right.

"But why?" Marcy said. "I thought…"

"I don't know. I just don't know," Red said.

They stood there for a little bit talking and exchanging apologies. Hal couldn't stop apologizing to Red. Now that he knew the truth, he was actually happy that she was dating him. So was Priscilla. She was glad that her daughter had found a lover with such a big cock. She also couldn't help but eye Brother Abernathy's sizable schlong as well.

Finally, Red took a look at the TV production area. "Brother Myrtlewood, it's time."

"What's he gonna do?" Priscilla asked Josie.

"He's gonna go on TV and tell everybody the truth."

Red, Brother Myrtlewood and Brother Abernathy turned and started walking towards the studio. This was it. There would be no going back after this.

"Brother Red! Wait!" A voice yelled from behind them.

They all turned. It was Brother Farlin and Gunter.

"We're sorry. We want to help," Gunter stammered as he nervously walked towards them. His guilt was obvious to everyone.

"But why, Gunter?" Josie said. "Why did you do it?"

Gunter shrugged. "I just wanted to fix my Audi."

Red looked at Brother Farlin who was as white as a sheet and so jittery that he couldn't stop fidgeting. Brother Abernathy walked over to him and punched him hard in the stomach. He crumpled like a dollar bill.

"I think you two had best be leaving."

Red ran over to them and pushed Brother Abernathy away.

"Stop it!" Red bent down and helped Brother Farlin up. He looked at Brother Abernathy sternly. "You know that there's room for everyone in this church."

Brother Farlin immediately began to weep. Gunter just wanted to fall through the floor.

"Brother Red, we're ready," Brother Myrtlewood said as he leaned out of the studio.

23

"Fuck her like you mean it!" Red said as Brother Abernathy shoved his big black cock deep into Josie's already stretched pussy.

Josie bit her lip as Brother Abernathy fucked her hard, doggie style. She moaned sharply with each thrust and gripped the sheets tightly. At the same time, she slurped up Brother Myrtlewood's cock and swallowed his pre-cum. Red was finding it hard to focus on her completely because he, in turn was fucking Marcy doggie style.

"Farlin, move in closer and get a shot of her face. I just love the way she looks when she's getting it hard."

Sister Gwen stood on the side watching and fingering herself to yet another massive orgasm. It was amazing how little things had changed since the news reports had come out. After all, here they were, at the Church, fucking their brains out, but now, they didn't care if anybody found out about them. Controversy was one of the most important tools *The Church of What's Happenin' Now* had its disposal when it came to spreading the good news.

Of course things had been a little dark there for a while immediately after Red had gone on the air telling the world about how he was a swinger and how he had just wanted to help people. He had told about his personal beliefs and apologized for acting one way and doing another. He had explained that he had only done this because he didn't expect people to understand and he didn't want to do anything to hurt the people he was most trying to help. He told them that he was just trying to give them what he thought they wanted. He told them how he was going to keep the church open and that the ministry was going to keep going as well. He said that his purpose in life was to help people and he was going to persevere even if he only had one person sitting in the congregation.

All the staff jumped ship except for Brother Abernathy, Brother Myrtlewood, Sister Gwen and Brother Farlin. It was only natural that people left the congregation in droves, as well, but some did stay. The ones who truly wanted to help people weren't bothered by the fact that their pastor was a sexually active man.

However, these people were in the minority. The attendance really dwindled and for a while it looked like Red was going to have to start selling the church's assets just to keep the charities going. He was on the verge of deciding to make the decision to sell the TV station, a funny thing started happening. People started attending the church again. It was a completely different group of people than the ones who had attended before. These people were open-minded and had been moved to hear him speak about his mission and how his church was for people without hang-ups. But moreover, because he didn't believe in judging people for what they did in their personal lives, but rather what they failed to do in regards to their fellow man. Maybe his congregation wasn't as big as it once was, but this time it was a lot more sincere. But perhaps, the real reason was that the church was now really about *What's Happenin' Now.*

Of course, with this new audience, Red realized that he could actually include his thoughts on sex in his messages. They were a big hit and it was then that Josie got the idea that Red should take his sex-positive message on the talk show circuit. She knew that they would be a success. Her relationship with Red had only gotten stronger through the turmoil.

Of course, she and Marcy kept their film careers outside the church going as well. Things were going so great that Josie was finally able to join Marcy as a *Solid Gold Medallion* contract girl. In fact, they were even able to get many people in the industry behind the church. They supported Red by making donations to the charities and helping him with his fundraisers. Even Gunter, whom Red had forgiven, was an active campaigner.

Red also easily forgave Brother Farlin for his betrayal. Especially after he realized that the aftermath of what had happened was really the best thing for him. He had to be honest with the world and more especially with himself. He was a swinger, plain and simple. Why should he hide something like that from the world? Didn't swingers need role models just like everybody else?

Another plus was that Red's writers block was gone and he was finally able to write the book he had always dreamed of, *The Man Who Could Shit Worlds.* It had been a bestseller for weeks, mostly due to his notoriety. Red was already half through the second draft of the follow up piece, *The Man Who Could Shit Gold.* He certainly wasn't any one trick pony, he would assure people of that.

Hal had even started working with the ministry, using his skills as a motivational speaker and self-help guru to give lectures and seminars on behalf of the church. He also poke to swingers groups and other sex friendly organizations.

Red moaned as Marcy bucked against him. That was another thing. Marcy was extremely satisfied since she had finally started sampling Red's big cock. There was no way she was going to stray from the fold now. Josie was a quivering mass as she fucked Brother Abernathy. He was stroking her hard and Brother Myrtlewood was thrusting his penis deep into her throat. After a minute, he changed his rhythm and Red could tell that he was shooting his load. Josie took a big swallow then began to concentrate on Brother Abernathy who was fucking her like a machine. Red picked up the pace on Marcy and couldn't resist slapping her on the ass as he banged her. She squealed and shuddered a bit as she came. He was amazed that he was able to keep from cumming himself. He looked at Sister Gwen over on the side fingering herself. Brother Farlin was going around snapping pictures and jerking off at the same time. Sister Gwen would give him a little suck now and again, just to give herself a little boost. She was too busy playing with herself to give him too much attention. Brother Abernathy then pulled out and shot a gigantic load into Josie's eager mouth, squirting so much that she had to swallow twice. Red then realized that he wasn't going to be able to take it any more.

"Fill me up!" Marcy said.

Red pumped her pussy full of his juice. He rammed it hard, thrusting it as deep as he could go. After he was finished, Sister Gwen crawled in bed and began to lick the cum out of Marcy's pussy.

Red just stood there staring. He then began to smile. He went over to Josie and gave her a big hug.

"Everything happens for a reason doesn't it?" He said.

"I guess that's why you had that dream," Josie said as she reached out and began to play with his penis.

"I guess so," Red said.

Josie turned serious for a minute. Something had been troubling her for months and she knew that she was going to have to bring it up eventually. Now seemed as good a time as any.

"Red, there's one thing we're gonna have to discuss."

"What's that?" Red said with a small sense of dread. He hoped that it wasn't anything serious.

"I know you like the black bra and panties, but I don't like wearing underwear. Can you see my dilemma?"

Red looked at her for a minute and then started laughing.

"Are you gonna still like me if I stop wearing them all the time?" Josie said a little nervously.

Red just kept laughing.

"I think I can manage," he said.